SUPERSTITIONS and APPARITIONS

The Sisters, Texas Mystery Series
Book 13

BECKI WILLIS

Editing by SJS Editorial Services
Cover by Diana Buidoso

ISBN 13: 978-1-947686-22-9

CONTENTS

1

"Maddy?"

Madison deCordova recognized the crackly voice on the other end of the line. Welcoming any excuse to avoid balancing the books for *In a Pinch Professional Services*, she greeted her caller with more enthusiasm than warranted. "Hello, Miss Virgie! How are you on this lovely day?"

"I'm finer than a frog's hair," her grandmother's lifelong friend replied. "Better than fine, fact be told." Like Granny Bert, she had a flair for dramatics. Pausing slightly for effect, she blurted out her big news, "I have us a case!"

The first thought through Madison's mind was *Us? When did Miss Virgie become a part of our team?* The second thought was *What kind of case? A temp job, or a nosing-around-and-getting-in-trouble case, the kind my husband highly frowns upon?*

"This one is a doozy, girl!" Virgie Adams proclaimed, her voice rising with excitement. "With a little negotiating, you can get top dollar for this one."

"Maybe you should tell me more about the job, first," Madison hedged. "What is it?"

In an innocent-sounding voice, the older woman assured her, "Just a little house sitting."

Madison was savvy enough to know that the about face in demeanor could only mean one thing. There was more—much more—to the story than Miss Virgie claimed. Like with Granny Bert, her innocent tone was all a ruse.

"If the client is willing to pay top dollar," Madison mused, "the house must be either sitting in the middle of a war zone or an alligator-infested swamp."

"Nope. It's in Manhattan."

Miss Virgie's excitement was suddenly contagious. It had been years since Madison last visited New York. The city should be vibrant with fall foliage now, dressed in its autumn best. Unless the homeowner insisted she stay at the house (most likely a high-rise apartment) around the clock, maybe she could take in a Broadway show and do some shopping. Christmas wasn't that long away. She couldn't splurge on anything big, but Bethani would love to have some small token from the city. Megan, too, she imagined. *Had her stepdaughter ever even been to New York?*

Reining in her excitement, Madison tried concentrating on the details of the job. "How long would I need to stay? And when do they need me?"

"The week of the next full moon. For the full week."

Madison drummed her fingers against her

chin. "Hmm. I'd have to consult a calendar to know when that is. And I'll have to check with Brash, of course, and see what the schedule looks like for the kids and *In a Pinch*. If there's no major obstacles in my way, and depending on plane tickets, I can probably squeeze it in. It's been a while since I've been to the Big Apple."

Her fingers were already flying across the keyboard. Seeing that the next full moon was only two weeks away—in her excitement, she didn't think to ask why a full moon mattered—she pulled up her preferred airline's website. She felt the bubble of excitement growing. If Brash was free, they could make it a romantic getaway to the city.

"The house is in Manhattan, not Big Apple," Virgie reminded her. "And I'm not sure what good plane tickets will do you. There's no airport in Manhattan."

"JFK and LaGuardia both service the city," Madison pointed out.

"Not that Manhattan. This house is in Manhattan, Texas."

And just like that, the bubble burst.

"Man—Manhattan, *Texas*?" The dismay was evident in her voice. Her fingers stilled on the keyboard, right along with her fanciful plans.

"That's right. It's about a half hour west of Big Apple."

"I've never heard of either."

"Manhattan is seventy or so miles northwest of Del Rio. I'd say it's a good six-hour drive. Close to four hundred miles due west of here, about halfway to El Paso."

Hearing no reply, Virgie persisted, "Maddy? You still there?"

"I'm here." The words sounded as lackluster as she felt.

"You remember Dom Hebert, my first husband's cousin. The one in Louisiana who claimed to have seen Benny Bodine alive." It wasn't a question. She knew Madison wouldn't forget the details surrounding Alpha Bodine's death anytime soon.

"Of course. I spoke to him by telephone."

"Well, it seems an uncle of his up and died, and left his estate to Dom. And just in case you're doing the math, I'll save you some time. Yes, the uncle was quite a bit younger than Dom's mother and, up until a few months ago, was still living."

"That explains that, then," Madison murmured. She guessed Dom was somewhere in his early seventies.

"Being from deep in Cajun country, Dom is all kinds of superstitious. Says he's seen firsthand what voodoo can do to a man, and he's not taking any chances on a house located at 1313 Omen Lane."

Madison was almost afraid to ask. "Where do I come in? What's he want me to do?"

"He wants you to stay in the house for a week and make certain it's safe."

"Safe?"

"Between the address and the urban legends, he's a bit spooked. Truth is, Dom always was a bit of a wuss," she scoffed.

"Not to sound like a parrot, but... urban legends? What urban legends?"

"Oh, the usual run of the mill ghost stories. Happened to a friend of a friend, that sort of thing." Virgie brushed aside the worry with a careless tone. "Glorified campfire stories. Nothing to be worried about, but you can't tell Dom that. He says there's too many coincidences. His uncle died on the seventh day of the seventh month. The address has the number thirteen in it not just once, but twice. Having *Omen* behind them doesn't help. I say he's just being a wuss, but he thinks it could be a sign of the devil." Madison could hear the eyeroll in Miss Virgie's voice.

Her own voice dry, Madison snarked, "Why, no. Asking me to be a human guinea pig isn't bothersome at all."

"He's offered to pay handsomely," the older woman reminded her, "as long as you agree to a handful of stipulations."

Madison bit back a groan. Granny Bert claimed life always came with stipulations. Complications, too. "Why does this already sound suspicious?"

"I don't know. Why does it?"

"It was a rhetor—never mind. I'll call Dom and get the conditions."

"No need. He gave them to me. Said he's headed out fishing and won't be by the phone for a few days."

Exasperated, Madison huffed out a deep breath. "Then how will we negotiate a price for the job?"

"Aw, that part's easy. He put me in charge of the negotiations."

"Fine. What's the top dollar he's willing to pay? Assuming I take the job, that's how much I want."

"Well, now, that's all fine and good," Virgie began. "But there's those stipulations to consider."

Madison had known there would be a snag. She may as well pull a thread now and know how bad it was. "Which are?"

"Like I said before. You have to stay seven days and seven nights."

Madison pursed her lips. "A bit oddly worded, but doable. Assuming my schedule is clear."

"You, or someone in your party, must remain on the property around the clock. At no point during that time shall the house be left unattended." It sounded as if she read from a script.

"Ooo-kay." *Weird, but still doable.*

"No matter what you see or hear, you or at least one person in your party must remain onsite, or all money due will be forfeited."

The threads tightened. "In that case, I'll require at least half the fee upfront."

"I told him as much, which he agreed to."

"Excellent. Anything else?"

"You aren't allowed to bring a cat, particularly a black one."

"No problem here. I don't own a cat."

"He's agreed to provide groceries and bottled water. The house will be stocked with basic foodstuffs, along with needed supplies. There's a charge account already set up at the nearest grocery store for anything else you might need."

The threads began to knot. "The house has a street address rather than a rural box number, but *nearest* implies it isn't exactly in town," Madison noted.

"You're right. It's about an hour from the outskirts of Manhattan."

"And how big is Manhattan?"

"Hard to say, as it's not incorporated, and most of the folks don't live within five miles of the town limits. But there's a post office, a big gas station with a liquor store and feed store all in one, and one grocery store and café."

"Sounds lovely."

The elderly woman ignored her sarcasm. "If you're fond of rocks, rattlesnakes, prickly pear and cactus, then I suppose it is."

The threads snarled into a snag. "You lost me at rattlesnakes."

"It's not like we don't have them here, you know," Virgie huffed. "Along with copperheads, water moccasin, coral sn—"

Instinctively, Madison lifted her feet a few inches off the ground. "Okay, okay. I get it. We have plenty of poisonous snakes in this part of Texas, too. Let's get back to the stipulations. What else?"

"You have to take me with you."

Surprise caused her to lower her feet, brow puckered. "He made that one of the stipulations?"

"Fine!" The older woman relented with a huff. "It was *my* stipulation. He wanted me to contact you and handle the details, so I added a stipulation of my own. I want to go along to investigate. And I want Bertha and Sybil with me. We made a good team before. We can do it again."

Even though her caller couldn't see it, Madison held up a staying hand. "Wait. First, you said he wanted me to house sit. Now, you're calling it an investigation. Which is it?"

"Why can't it be both? Investigate while staying at the house." Ever practical, Virgie reasoned, "Less overhead, more time to concentrate. We can really get the *feel* of the case that way."

Madison was more confused than ever. "What case? What am I supposedly investigating? And when did you and Miss Sybil—even Granny Bert, for that matter—become a part of the *In a Pinch* team?"

"With Genny out tending her babies, we figure you're short-handed."

"You do realize Genny doesn't work for me, right? *New Beginnings* keeps her more than busy."

"I'm not talking about your temporary services, and you know it. I'm talking about the *other* job you do. Bertha helps you out plenty of times. And you have to admit, the four of us made a good team at Alpha's."

"You did." Madison gave her that much. Her geriatric sidekicks even collected part of the reward. "But you still haven't told me what I'm investigating."

"Well, now, that's the kicker." At Virgie's hesitant tone, Madison felt another snag. "He's not quite sure," the older woman admitted. "That's why he wants to hire you."

"And you think it requires you, my grandmother, and Miss Sybil to get to the bottom of it?"

She could practically hear the shrug on the other end of the line. "It can't hurt."

"What does Mr. Hank think about this? Won't he mind if you go off for a week without him?"

Miss Virgie's snort of derision came through loud and clear. "Are you kidding? He'll see it as a vacation of his own. He can watch all the television and eat all the cold pizza he can handle. I try to limit both, you know, because of his rheumatism and cholesterol. Sittin' around, eating all those carbs isn't good for him, but a week here and there won't kill him."

"Still, I think he would want to go with you..."

"Not to the ranch, he won't! You may not know this about my Hank, but he's got a jealous streak. He doesn't like to be reminded of my first husband, and the house is part of the Perkins Ranch, which belonged to Robert's family."

"Cattle ranch or horses?"

"A few cows and goats, but mostly exotic game. Hunting is a big thing down there."

"According to my guys, it's a big thing here, too," Madison said dryly. Both her husband and her eighteen-year-old son were enthralled with the sport.

"Maybe you could negotiate a deal for a hunting trip out of this, seeing as you had to reveal Brash's Christmas present a few months too early."

Virgie dangled the bait without shame.

In spite of herself, Madison was intrigued. "That is a thought."

She and Brash had a sort of competition going, seeing which one could give the best gift without spending a lot of money. Her intended present for him this year, a pair of exceptionally well-painted Western canvases, played a vital role in a thirty-year-old murder cold case she helped investigate. She had no choice but to reveal them as evidence and had been searching for a suitable replacement ever since. A hunting trip to West Texas might be just the thing.

"If I throw in a hunting trip for Brash, will you take the job?" Virgie pressed.

"Why are you so eager for me to take this job?"

"I only went to the ranch two times, but I'd like to see it again before I die."

"Even if Mr. Hank doesn't go?"

"I know you and Brash are barely more than newlyweds, but Hank and I have been married for over fifty years. As much as I love the man, sometimes we both need a little break. I figure this gives us time away from each other, I can see the ranch again, the girls and I can help you make certain the house is safe to live in, and you can make a nice little piece of change in the process."

"I don't even know what kind of fee he's willing to pay."

Virgie named a price that sent the bubbles of excitement percolating again.

"Just to *house sit*?" Maddy asked, eyes wide.

"And investigate."

Madison considered it for only a moment. A job paying that well would make balancing her checkbook so much more pleasant. Plus, if she could snag a couple of hunts out of the deal, it made it all the sweeter...

"Before I say yes, I have a few stipulations of my own."

"Of course. What are they?"

"First, I don't know if Brash will go along with this rather sketchy-sounding proposition. The chance to do a few days of hunting may entice him to join us. I want permission for him to hunt while we're at the house."

"It's already arranged."

Maddy's surprise sounded in her voice. "It is?"

"I figured he'd tag along, if for no reason other than to protect me and Sybil from any trouble you and Bertha get into. He expects the two of you to stir up some dust, but Sybil and I are still on his good side."

Glossing over the implication that she and Granny Bert were on her husband's 'bad' side, Maddy continued, "Fine. But I want a second hunting trip, too, for next year. I can give it to him to replace the paintings."

"I'm sure that's no problem. Anything else?"

"I probably should have asked this first. Is the house livable?"

"The uncle lived there until his death this summer."

"I don't know how many rooms it has, but I

want a private bedroom."

"Absolutely."

"Is there cell phone service and Wi-Fi there?"

"It's spotty and somewhat unreliable, but it's there."

Unable to think of additional stipulations, Madison blew out a breath. "Let me talk to Brash, and I'll get back with you."

Virgie Adams' response sounded confident. "I'll start packing!"

2

"Let me get this straight. A client wants you to spend a week in a house to make certain it's 'safe?'" Brash deCordova used air quotes after hearing his wife's latest job proposition.

"That's the way I understand it."

"Safe from the roof falling in?" the law officer asked. "Safe from vandals? Safe from the pack of raccoons living in the attic?"

Madison grimaced. "I certainly hope none of those are the case."

"Then what harm, exactly, are you checking for?"

"From what I gather, he's afraid the house may be ... haunted, for lack of a better word."

Brash's brow crooked with his infamous look. The gesture was half frown, half arched eyebrow. Nostrils slightly flared. The expression had served him well as a college football coach, stern father, and now officer of the law. Most people were intimidated by the look, but not his wife.

"Haunted?" he questioned.

Madison tucked her long legs beneath her as they sat on the porch swing in the crisp autumn night, enjoying cups of hot apple cider.

"Haunted, cursed, something like that," she said with a nod. "It seems Dom Hebert is very superstitious, and the house sits at 1313 Omen Lane. The uncle who willed him the house died on the seventh day of the seventh month." Madison blew on her drink before taking a cautious sip. "I don't know. Maybe a hawk flew over at high noon and cast a shadow. Anyway. For whatever reason, he suspects the house may be haunted. He says all the signs point to evil. Something along those lines."

"Signs?"

"Thirteen-thirteen. Seven-seven. That's why I need to stay for seven days and seven nights. On the week of a full moon."

"I see."

It was clear he didn't.

"Oh, and there was something about some urban legend. A glorified campfire tale, Miss Virgie called it."

"Yet she wants to go along."

"Not only that, she wants Granny Bert and Miss Sybil to be a part of it."

"The geriatric crew rides again," Brash said, nudging his shoulder into hers. He wore a mischievous grin upon his handsome face.

"I suppose they're looking for another girls trip," she mused.

"It's been about seven decades since any of

them have been *girls.* At least they aren't taking Miss Wanda along. She'd really stir things up."

"Granny Bert has already started packing, and I haven't even agreed to take the job yet."

"But you're thinking you may." It wasn't a question.

"I don't think I can afford *not* to. He's paying an outrageous price. You know the seven-seven thing?"

Brash's eyes widened, his voice incredulous. "He's paying you seven grand to house sit for a week?"

"No. He's paying me seven thousand, seven hundred, and seventy-seven dollars to house sit for a week."

Brash let out a low whistle. "That's some serious cash. What's the catch?"

"Other than the whole haunted house of the devil thing? If I or someone in my party doesn't occupy the property the entire seven days and seven nights, I forfeit the money."

"You'll need to demand half the money upfront."

"Already done."

Madison felt his broad shoulder lift with a shrug. "That's still almost four thousand dollars," her husband noted. "Not too shabby for a week's work."

"Oh, I intend to stay for the full term," she assured him. "Between all of us, surely we can manage round-the-clock occupancy."

With their cider mugs emptied, Brash

gathered her into his arms and snuggled his face into her hair. "I'm not sure I can go an entire week without you. I hope it's close enough I can sneak over for a mid-week visit."

After a seductive and lingering kiss, Madison pulled her thoughts back together. "That's the thing. It's in Manhattan. And before you jump to the same misguided conclusions I did, that's Manhattan, Texas, not New York. About six hours west of here."

"So roughly halfway to El Paso." His mouth turned down in disapproval as he continued, "and much too close to the border for comfort."

"But it pays $7,777," Madison reminded him. "Plus, there's a nice little bonus you'll be interested in."

"To snag my interest, it will have to be a big bonus."

"We've arranged for you to go along and hunt for the week. The house is in the middle of a game ranch."

Brash was quiet for a moment. "Deer hunt?" There was no denying the interest in his voice.

Nodding, Madison sweetened the deal. "Mule deer, white-tail, and axis. I hear they have some real trophies in that part of the state."

"You know it." After a moment of contemplation, he asked, "When is this assignment?"

"The next full moon, which is two weeks away."

"I'd have to clear my schedule. And we have to make certain the kids are okay with it. I'm sure my parents would be thrilled to have them there for the week."

Madison visibly brightened. "I hadn't thought of that! I'm still not used to the twins having normal, loving grandparents for a change. My parents are much too flighty, and Gray's parents are much too rigid. Your parents are the perfect mix of the two. Firm but fun."

"I'll check my schedule and get with them first thing in the morning."

"So, you'll go?"

"I wouldn't be comfortable with you going without me. Not only is there the way you and your grandmother always manage to get into trouble, but that's a remote and potentially dangerous part of the country."

"I hear there's rattlesnakes."

"And theirs are bigger than ours."

Madison covered her ears. "Would everyone stop reminding me that we have rattlesnakes in the Brazos Valley? I prefer to think of them as a West Texas sort of thing."

"You know there's rattlers on the coast, too, right?"

"And just like that, you ruined my plans for a summer vacation on the beach."

"Sorry, babe." Laughing, Brash pulled her closer. "How about if I walk in front of you and carry a big stick?"

Madison sank against his warm, protective body. "When we go to Manhattan, you'd better be packing a gun. I'm not taking any chances on close encounters with rattling reptiles or anything else."

Tightening his hold on her, he promised to keep her as safe as humanly possible. Maddy lay her head on his shoulder and listened to the strong, steady beat of his heart.

She was half asleep when Brash murmured into her hair, "It's the *anything else* that has me worried."

"Hot dang, we're going to Manhattan!"

Bertha Hamilton Cessna, affectionately known as Granny Bert and considered the town matriarch, rubbed her arthritic hands together and beamed across the table at Madison.

"I take it you're excited?" Madison mused, humored by her grandmother's reaction.

"Darn tooting, I am! It's been quite a spell since I've been to that part of the country. It's hard land but has a beauty all its own. Doesn't hurt that that's where the television series *Rattled* is filmed."

"Really? I didn't know that." Madison twisted her lips. "Come to think of it, I didn't know there was even a series called *Rattled*."

"Sure. It's about a family who catches and rehabs injured or trapped rattlesnakes. The whole family does it, even the little eight-year-old girl."

A shiver of revulsion shook Maddy's shoulders. "First, why would anyone let their eight-year-old anywhere near a venomous snake? Second, why would you, or anyone else for that matter, want to watch such a revolting thing? And third, why would someone rehab a snake, particularly a rattler? I say kill every one of them!"

"Snakes are important to the ecosystem. And the timber rattler, or canebrake rattler as some call it, is a protected species. You'd best not kill it. Besides, the show is very entertaining. Sticker is especially fond of it."

"Speaking of Sticker, what does he say about you going off for a week?"

"What does it matter? He has no say in the matter. I'm my own woman," her eighty-two-year-old grandmother huffed in defiance.

"Of course."

"I'm sure Arlene's sister-in-law Jolene Kopetsky will be more than happy to keep him company while I'm gone."

"I don't think you have anything to worry about, Granny. That man worships the ground you walk on."

"Maybe so, but his boots have a way of wanderin' around every chance they get."

"How can you say that?"

"How can I not? The old coot's been married so many times, he's reaching the legal limit."

"I don't think he's quite there yet. I think he's only been married six or so times. And all of those were while you were married to, or still mourning, Grandpa Joe."

"I'm still mourning him!" her grandmother snapped. "He was the love of my life and don't you forget it."

"I haven't. Everyone knows how happy the

two of you were. But it's okay if you want to finally accept Sticker's marriage proposal. It's good to move on with your life."

"I agree, so let's move on out of this conversation and get back to our trip. I think Wanda may go with us."

Madison couldn't help but blink in surprise. "Since when?"

"Since we told her we were going, and she asked to go along. Think about it. It will even things out so no one will be left rolling around like a fifth wheel. Two people can stay at the house at all times, while the others go out and about."

Madison had to admit the idea did hold merit. But in normal Granny Bert fashion, her grandmother chose to seek forgiveness rather than ask permission. *Come to think of it, she didn't even seek forgiveness. She just barreled her way right in.*

Hedging, Madison pointed out, "We don't even know the size or layout of the house. There may not be enough beds."

"I'll take a blow-up mattress, just in case you and Brash need it."

"You want Brash and me to take the blow-up?" she asked, somewhat taken aback by the suggestion.

"Now that you've offered, I think it would probably be for the best. You two are the youngest, and, being the Southern gentleman that he is, I know Brash will insist."

Madison didn't bother arguing; there was no winning against Granny Bert. Simply trying was exhausting. Instead, she changed the subject.

"I wish I knew what to expect. I don't know a thing about the house."

"It has five bedrooms, so we're good."

Again blinking in surprise, Madison asked, "How do you know that?"

Granny Bert shrugged. "I know someone."

"Of course you do," the younger woman muttered.

"A friend of mine knew the uncle and took food when he was ailing. She told me all about the house."

"What did she say?"

"Like I said, five bedrooms. Not sure if all have beds, so I figured I'd pack the blow-up, just in case. At least two bathrooms. As long as Wanda doesn't eat Chinese, that should be enough."

Madison grimaced. "Thank you for that information."

"Virgie said that when they go to stock the house, they'll change sheets, sweep, mop, that sort of thing."

"Do we know if there's internet?" Her tone was hopeful.

"Don't hold your breath. The ranch is a good thirty or forty miles from a one-horse town. You're lucky there's electricity and a landline."

All pretense of enthusiasm was gone. "This assignment just gets better and better," Maddy sulked.

"Virgie says you're being paid well enough to rough it for a few days."

"I suppose. Speaking of pay, where did Dom get his money? That's a rather substantial amount for such a small job."

"If everything checks out, and he accepts his inheritance, he stands to make a pretty penny," Granny Bert informed her. "It's more than just the house. It's over two hundred acres, a stake in the ranch profits, and a percentage of the oil rights. Between the three, it comes to a sizable income."

"And if he doesn't accept?"

"Virgie says if anything strange is going on, he's superstitious enough to think he dodged a bullet and will probably still consider it money well spent."

"I'm still a little fuzzy on what I'm supposed to be doing. What does he consider *strange*?"

"My understanding is that he'll provide a packet for you at the house with full details."

"That sounds rather mysterious."

"Sybil met him once, the time she and Alpha went down to the Louisiana swamps to find that good-for-nothing Lester Bodine, after he skipped out on Alpha. She recalls that Dom was a bit high strung. At the time, he was convinced Marie Laveau had come back from the dead and haunted his family for something they'd done in the past. It sounds like he hasn't calmed down much with age."

"No, it doesn't."

"If nothing else, it should be interesting," her grandmother declared.

Interesting, indeed.

3

Madison was a huge fan of the famed Texas 'Hill Country.' It hardly seemed fitting that this visit was so brief. Other than stopping for gas, snacks, and a bathroom break, the only sightseeing they did was by windshield.

The further west they traveled, the rockier the terrain. Towns shrank in size and were spaced further apart.

Calling the Brazos Valley home, she was accustomed to gently rolling hills, plenty of trees, and lush green fields, fertile from river-bottom soil.

Here, the hills rose into jagged limestone formations, and the trees became shorter and squatter. The brittle land was flatter than she was used to, edged with bluffs capped and cropped with sharp, rugged plateaus. An occasional oak tree offered leafy respite to the pointed needles of shrubby cedars and juniper, and an over-abundance of mesquite thorns.

It seemed everything out here included a sharp point, including the horned toads, free-range goats, and aoudads.

"How much longer until we get there?" Wanda Shanks wanted to know.

"Fifteen minutes less than the last time you asked," Madison replied. To herself, she thought, *Geesh! She's worse than the twins used to be!*

"Why does Virgie get to ride with that good-looking husband of yours? His music is better than yours," the older woman complained.

"You've all taken turns riding in Brash's truck," she pointed out.

A smile tickled Madison's mouth as she recalled her husband's lackluster enthusiasm over travel arrangements. As previously agreed, the four older women alternated riding shotgun with him after each restroom stop. Troubles ensued when they squabbled over uneven times and 'deliberate manipulation' of the system. Someone accused Wanda of making a fraudulent emergency stop to hasten her turn in the truck, a fact she vehemently denied. To the lawman's horror, she went into great detail of her delicate digestive system and how certain foods affected her.

If any of the very outspoken women had ever had a filter governing what was considered 'appropriate' conversation for mixed company, it was long gone by now. Poor Brash was now the recipient of unwanted insight into the aging process. Recalling his expression at the last rest stop and passenger switch still amused her.

Hoping her teasing tone explained the smile, she asked, "Why? Is my driving that bad?"

"Do you really want us to answer that?" Granny Bert huffed from the backseat. "You drive like a widow woman!"

"Technically, I am," she reminded her grandmother. "Or I was, before my marriage to Brash. Besides, what's that even supposed to mean? And might I remind you that all three of you are widows, as well, and I don't hear you complaining about each other's driving."

"Not mine, you don't. But there's a reason we don't let Sybil drive."

Beside her, her best friend offered a mild protest. "I resent that!"

"You know it's true. You have your strong points, but driving isn't one of them. Remember that time you went down a one-way street in the middle of Dallas, going the wrong direction? We had more horns blowing at us than there are in the New York and Boston orchestras put together!"

"I needed to go in that direction," Sybil maintained stubbornly. "Is it my fault the roads in the city are all turned around and don't make any sense?"

"She's right about that," Wanda agreed. "The worst are those roundabouts. I go in complete circles a time or two before I figure out how and where to get off."

Madison had no such problem here. With Fredericksburg behind them, there was nothing but highway ahead. It rose and fell with the staggered elevations but held true to its westward trek. She drove as her three passengers recalled travel adventures and near mishaps. Tuning them out as best possible and thankful they were now laughing instead of arguing, she wondered what they would encounter upon reaching the house. Her idea of suitable living conditions could differ from someone else's. Plus, she couldn't help but think there was a catch since Dom Hebert was so willing to pay top dollar for this assignment. What hadn't he told them?

By the time they rolled into Manhattan, the community was settled in for the night. The post office had been closed for hours, and the small grocery store with attached café closed a half hour ago, ending their hopes of a hot meal before heading to the ranch.

Hungry, tired, and out of sorts, the two-vehicle caravan stopped at *Jackrabbit's*, the only other business in town. The feed store portion had closed at five, and the rest would shut down at ten, leaving only the outside gas pumps in service overnight.

If the signs outside were to be believed, *Jackrabbit's* served hot, fresh pizza, golden fried chicken, and an assortment of deli sandwiches. Tonight, the only choices were three slices of reheated pizza, a few shriveled up wings and legs, and two questionable-looking ham sandwiches with soggy bread and wilted vegetables. Brash told the cashier to ring them all up, along with chips and drinks and a few bananas that were a day or two past their prime. Adding packaged pastries and cookies to their bag, he paid for their 'dinner' before asking whose turn it was to ride with him.

Four wrinkled hands shot into the air.

"One word of warning. The food rides in the Expedition."

One by one, the hands lowered.

"Oh, fine," Granny Bert grumbled. "You gluttons ride with Maddy. I'll starve along with Brash."

"No one is going to starve," Madison chastised. "Brash, take your pick. You can have mine, too. I'll eat when we reach the house."

"That will be at least an hour from now, maybe longer. It's almost dark, and it will be harder to see where we're going." He shot a glance toward the three primary reasons for the considerable delay. The women were too busy complaining about... well, everything... to notice him hand the bag to Granny Bert for her selection. "I had planned to be there already."

"It can't be helped now," Maddy sighed. "I'll have a bag of chips to tide me over."

"Take a banana, too, although you may have to fight the fruit flies for every bite." He brushed a kiss across her lips, advised her to be safe and follow close behind, and handed her the bag of food. "See you there."

An hour and fifteen minutes later, their headlights skipped over the rough gravel road posing as Omen Lane. To Madison's limited view, it looked little more than a trail. The dwindling daylight made seeing anything more than general shapes difficult. With every bump and every grump, light slowly leaked from the day.

There were only two houses on Omen Lane. The first was a burned-out shell with a tree growing through its roof. Against the backdrop of the faintly lit sky, the silhouette provided the perfect image for a haunted house.

The only other house on the lane was a close contender.

It wasn't derelict abandon that made the house so formidable. Nor was it the superstitions surrounding its house number, 1313. It wasn't the lifeless, baron yard, nor the rickety picket fence encircling its perimeter. It wasn't even the way it loomed large and baleful against the skyline.

Madison couldn't say exactly what it was about the house that sent a shiver of dread rippling down her spine. But something about the overwhelming *grayness* of the house—from the concrete bricks and stone steps to the weathered siding and paint-peeled porch posts—made for an ominous presence. Gray might be all the rage in interior design these days, but too much was depressing. It didn't help that nightfall darkened the hues and created exaggerated shadows.

She started to follow Brash into the driveway, but he motioned her to stop. He stuck his head out the window to call, "I want to back in. You may want to, too."

Even though he never said the words aloud, she knew why Brash wanted them to back in. It was in case they needed to make a quick getaway.

The shiver crawled further down her spine. As she rolled up her window, she imagined the word *sinister* floated in the air.

And I agreed to seven nights and seven days in this house!

She forced more enthusiasm into her voice than she felt. "Ladies, it seems we've finally arrived!"

"Thank the good Lord for small favors! My bladder is about to bust!" Wanda proclaimed. Her door was already half-open.

"Sure doesn't look like much," Virgie grunted. "I hope this is worth all the fuss, not to mention the expense Dom is going to."

Wanda stopped midway out the door. "That's right," she remembered. "Bertha was vague about the money. What does this trip pay?"

Madison's bright demeanor never wavered. "A week's vacation! All expenses paid."

Wanda looked to the house, forlorn and glum in the harsh headlights, back at Madison, and shrugged. "I've worked for less," she concluded.

Madison wasn't sure about how much work Wanda and the other octogenarians would do, but she was thankful there was no grumbling over the pay, or, in this case, the lack thereof.

"Why don't you ladies wait while I get the house opened and the lights on?" Brash suggested.

"If I wait much longer, I think we'll all regret it," Wanda insisted. She hustled behind Brash to the front door.

Dom had mailed them the key, so Brash

inserted it into the lock and turned the handle. He had no more found the light switch and stepped through the threshold with caution when Wanda barreled her way past him.

"If you find the powder room before me, let me know. I'm headed yonder way!" She pointed toward a hall that led off the main room.

For a woman of her age and bulk, Brash was impressed with how quickly she moved.

"So much for securing the house before the ladies came in," he muttered aloud.

After Madison backed the Expedition in, she and the others dredged in at a slower pace, their joints stiff and their limbs achy after a long day of travel. Granny Bert and Virgie had their arms full of purses, sweaters, knitting bags, and the like, while Sybil carried in the takeout bags and other trash. Madison pulled up the rear, carrying an overnight bag on each shoulder, along with her computer bag.

"You ladies drop your stuff here while I look around. Miss Wanda didn't want to wait, but why don't the rest of you check out the kitchen?" Brash suggested. He reached past his wife to lock the front door and asked her in a low voice. "Is your car locked?"

"Yes. I double checked."

"Good. I'll get the rest of our things later. Try to keep the ladies in the kitchen until I give you the all clear."

His serious tone flagged her concern. "Is something wrong?"

"I'll just feel better if you're all in one spot," he

said, avoiding directly answering the question. "I'll go check out the rest of the house."

Madison took a moment to ease the pucker from her brow. While prepping her poker face before joining the other women, she surveyed the room.

Nothing to write home about. Typical seventies-style furniture, other than the newish recliner and television. Plenty of avocado green and harvest gold for that authentic nostalgic look. At least it's clean. Not as bad as it could be, she concluded.

She headed off to the kitchen to find the others.

"Turn on those faucets," she heard her grandmother directing someone. "No telling how long it's been since those pipes have seen fresh water. Don't be surprised if the hot water smells like rotten eggs."

"Hopefully, they flushed it all out when they cleaned the house," Virgie responded. She peered inside the pantry. "Seems stocked well enough. All the staples, plus a few extras."

"Same in the frig," Sybil reported. "Milk, eggs, butter, and cheese. Some lunch meats and condiments."

"All the dishes and utensils we'll need," Granny Bert added. She paused while inspecting drawers and cupboards to retrieve a piece of paper taped on one door. "Here's a note that says we'll find a couple of casseroles in the back freezer, ready to thaw and bake. We're to help ourselves to anything we find in there."

Sybil nodded. "We'll need to take full inventory in the morning so we can make a shopping list. At least we can make eggs and toast for breakfast."

A rustling sound came from the hallway. "Whew!" Wanda proclaimed as she bustled in. "What a relief. My eyeballs were floating for the past thirty minutes."

Not long afterward, Brash joined the women.

"I made a quick tour of the house. All the bedrooms are upstairs, except for one small space that has an ancient computer and a half bed. The four upstairs bedrooms are large and airy, and there's two full baths, as well. I suggest we all stay up there if everyone is able to take the stairs."

Granny Bert leveled him a hard glare. "Surely, you aren't implying that we're old."

"Never," he assured her. "I don't know about any of you, but I have a trick knee that sounds like popcorn when I do a lot of stairs. I'm just asking if anyone has any concerns about taking the staircase each day."

"At our ages, we have concerns about everything," Virgie assured him. She spoke for the group as a whole. "It will make it cozier if we all stay together. Right, girls?"

A chorus of agreement rose in the air.

"Upstairs it is," Madison confirmed. "I'll help bring in the bags."

"No need."

"I insist." Her firm voice allowed no argument.

"On second thought, that may be a good idea."

She had no illusions that his sudden about-face was credited to her taking a stand. He had another reason. For some inexplicable reason, the hairs at the back of her neck stood on end.

She waited until they reached the front door to question him. Before she said a word, her fears were confirmed when Brash took a pistol from the back of his belt and pressed it into her hands.

"I'll go out, you stay here near the house. Keep a flashlight and the gun handy."

"Brash, what is going on?"

"Hopefully, nothing," he replied. The stern lines around his mouth said otherwise. "That's why I wanted to get here before dark. I don't know the lay of the land, the dynamics of the people, anything. I just know we're in potentially dangerous territory, and I don't want any surprises. Keep one eye on the door, the other on me. Don't let anyone slip inside while we're out here."

"I'll just lock the door."

"No. I don't want you wasting time if you need to get back in."

She resented his implication. "Like I'd leave you out here to fend for yourself!" Madison huffed.

"If it were just the two of us, it would be one thing. But we have those four in there to think about."

"Hang on. I'll get Granny Bert to stand guard at the door."

From behind them, her grandmother spoke. "No need to fetch me. I'm right here."

After a half-yelped start, Madison's fear

melted into relief. "Where did you come from?"

"I told the girls I had to visit the powder room. I came to see what you two were up to."

Brash nodded his approval. "I'm going out to get the bags. You can stay here at the door, and Maddy can be sentry at the corner of the house. I'll bring the rifles in first, so you'll be armed, too."

"Already am," the old woman grinned, producing a Glock 43. "We'll watch your back."

Again, Brash nodded his approval. There would be no hiding the light spilling from within the vehicles, so he flipped on his tactical flashlight as he stepped off the porch and into the darkness.

Madison waited nervously on the porch, scanning the yard for any signs of movement. She didn't breathe easy until he was back on the porch with the first load. Brash locked the vehicle behind him with each trip, of which there were several. As promised, the hunting rifles came in first.

Once everything was in the house and the vehicle alarms set, Brash locked the front door behind them. He slid the chain latch and engaged the deadbolt for added security.

"Round up the others and let's call it a night," he suggested. "It's not that late, but I know we're all beat."

"They've already started up with some of the luggage," Granny Bert informed him, motioning to the dwindling pile. "We saved the heavier ones for you."

They had the luggage upstairs and the rooms assigned in short order. Wanda and Virgie took one room, with Sybil and Granny Bert in another. A Jack-and-Jill bathroom connected the two. Wanda giggled and said it would be like a sleepover.

An identical setup was across the hallway, of which Brash chose the front bedroom as theirs. Madison knew it wasn't about the best mattress but about the best view of the entrance.

"I found the packet of information Dom promised, but I say let's save it for the morning. I'll be the first to admit that those ladies wore me out today." Brash had no shame over the fact.

"Thank you for being such a good sport about all this." Madison brushed a smile across his lips.

"They wore me out, too. You only had one at a time. I had three!"

"Let's get a good night's sleep and worry about everything else when we can think straight."

"And I'm sure the house won't look so imposing in the light of day." It was clear that Madison tried to convince herself with the words.

"At least we didn't see a black cat walk under a ladder," her husband offered.

She rolled her eyes as she crawled beneath the sheets. "I'm too tired to comment on that, other than to say you're not helping."

"With all the thirteens floating around, I thought it was worth a shot." He punched the pillow to shape it to his liking. "Good night, sweetheart. Love you."

"Love you, too. I hope you sleep well."

Within minutes, they both were sound asleep. Sometime past midnight, they were abruptly awakened as a woman's high-pitched wail pierced the night.

4

Already flinging the covers back, Brash warned in an urgent whisper, "Stay here!"

He was on his feet, gun and light in hand, before Madison could form a coherent thought.

Her mind cleared, and she immediately thought of her grandmother. "Granny Bert!" she whispered in alarm as she, too, jumped from bed. "I'm going with you. What if one of the ladies fell down the stairs?"

It was faster to relent than argue. "Grab a light and stay close behind me. Don't make a peep."

"Do I need a gun?" She wasn't fond of handling one, but sometimes, necessity required it. What if a rattlesnake had crawled into the bed with one of the older women? What if a vagrant had secretly lived in the attic while the house was unattended?

Brash answered before her imagination could run rampant. "Wouldn't hurt."

Together, they tiptoed to the door and peered into the darkness beyond. Other than the loud tick of an ancient clock downstairs, there was only silence.

Seconds later, Granny Bert opened her bedroom door. "What in tarnation was that?" she hissed in a loud whisper.

The other door cracked open, and Miss Virgie rushed out, a nightcap on her head and her pajamas askew. The sound of Wanda's snore thrummed in tune with the tension pulsing in the hall.

"What was that?" Virgie demanded, keeping her voice low.

"It wasn't one of you?" Brash asked. He hadn't thought so, but he needed to be certain.

"Didn't come from our room. You can tell that Wanda is dead to the world."

"Sybil, too. Sleeping on her good ear," Granny Bert confirmed.

"Keep the lights off and a flashlight handy but peek out all the windows. Don't open the curtains if you can help it. No direct light. Watch for movement below. Maddy, you check this side of the house. I'm going down."

"Not without me, you're not!" Madison objected.

"Fine. Granny, you take this side of the hall. Miss Virgie, you take that one. Stay here until we get back."

"You're not going outside, are you?" Granny Bert asked in alarm.

"There's a difference in being a brave fool and a dead one. I don't know anything about the property or where anything is. I'm not planning to explore it now in the dark. I'll make certain the house is secure and go from there."

"What's the signal if there's a problem?" Virgie wanted to know.

"You'll know it if you hear it," Brash assured her grimly. With a motion of his dark head, just barely visible in the low light, he indicated for his wife to follow.

They moved stealthily down the creaking steps. With excruciating precision, Brash found just the right place to put their weight so that they descended as quietly as possible. Once on the ground floor, he stayed her with his hand so that their eyes could adjust to a different kind of darkness. Here, new light glowed in tiny bursts of green or blue, confirming electronic connections but creating fuzzy halos that could play tricks on the eyes. Faint moonlight peeked through a slit in the living room curtains and around the front door.

Madison made a mental note to put a towel beneath the threshold. The small effort might dissuade snakes from joining them inside.

Hearing only the annoying tick of the clock and seeing no movement from within, Brash used body language to tell Madison to stay in place. He slipped across the room to check each window, careful not to disturb the curtains. Satisfied that the windows remained locked, and no one had blindsided him, he moved back to Madison and pulled her along into the hall.

He paused at each room to repeat the process. Madison hovered close behind, watching over their shoulders and for shifting shadows.

With all entrances and exits secure, Brash

turned on his flashlight and directed Madison to do the same, his voice little more than a breath in her ear.

"Keep the beam low and away from the windows. No need letting anyone out there know our whereabouts, or even that we're awake."

They searched room by room, checking all potential hiding spots, before moving back up to the second floor.

"What took so long?" Granny Bert wanted to know. "We've searched all the closets and under all the beds. The only place we didn't check is the attic."

"Where are the steps?"

"Pull-down steps there at the end of the hall."

Brash pushed past the women to shine his light upward. He returned with a report. "Taped shut to keep out a draft. Looks like it's overgrown with dust, so I think it's safe."

"Now what?" Virgie asked, stifling a yawn.

"Go back to sleep. I'll make myself comfy here at the top of the stairs."

"I'll spell you at dawn," Granny Bert promised. She was already turning back toward her room, as was her friend.

Alone in the hall, Madison slipped her arm through Brash's. "I'll stay with you."

"Nonsense. One of us may as well get some sleep."

"I doubt there will be much more sleeping tonight," she said in a rueful voice.

"At least try. I'll get the blanket from the empty bedroom and settle in here."

"I'll get it all. There's a chair in our room you can pull out here to sit in."

Five minutes later, they had Brash a semi-decent place to spend the rest of the night. No one could step onto the second floor without getting past him.

"I'm sorry, sweetheart," Madison said, placing a regretful kiss upon his lips.

"Hey, it could be worse." His smile had a way of making everything better. "More than likely, it was a cougar. The female's cry sounds like a woman screaming, but I think we'll all sleep better knowing I'm on guard."

"All of us," she pointed out. "Not you."

"I'll catch a few winks here and there. If not, I'll let Granny Bert take over."

"Promise?"

"Promise. Get some rest, sweetheart."

"I'll try." She kissed her husband again. "Let me know if you see or hear anything, or if you need a break. I love you."

"Love you, too. Now go to bed."

Madison turned with reluctance, feeling guilty for having the bed to herself while her husband's large form was stuffed into a lumpy armchair. She crawled beneath the covers and waited for sleep to come. After squirming and tossing, and willing her mind into a blank state, it was obvious her efforts were in vain.

The room dark, she made her way to the window and carefully peeled back the curtain. With her eyes already adjusted to the night, it was easier to pick out shapes by the dim glow of the waxing gibbous moon. She made out a few trees and squat shrubs, and in the distance, the ridge of a ragged rock formation.

Madison studied the silhouette, idly wondering if the wind was stronger at that elevation. The spindly trees atop the plateau appeared to sway steadily to the right. She shifted her eyes to the trees nearer the house, seeing no such movement.

Odd, she thought, watching the persistent bent atop the ridge. She grew bored after a while, and her gaze wandered. The yard and surrounding area were still and quiet. It seemed the whole world slumbered, herself and Brash excluded.

Knowing it was best that one of them be semi-rested, Madison once again crawled into bed.

A long while later, sleep came.

When Madison awoke, Brash's warm body lay next to hers. She glorified in the feel of his nearness for a moment before moving stealthily from the bed. She was almost to the bathroom door when his sleep-roughened voice said, "Wake me in an hour."

"I will," she promised. "Go back to sleep."

She dressed quickly and exited through the opposite door of the Jack-and-Jill setup. Stepping from the other bedroom, she saw her grandmother still stationed at the top of the stairs, shotgun in hand.

"'Morning," Madison said in a low voice as she approached. "Everyone else still in bed?"

"So far. If you're ready for coffee, I'll go down with you. It's full daylight now, so we can see if anyone is out and about and up to no good."

Madison noted that her grandmother didn't relinquish her gun as the two moved quietly down the steps.

After peering out the window to make certain both vehicles were still in the drive, Madison found the coffee pot and a fresh can of coffee. Unfamiliar with that brand of brewer and unsure of the right portions to use, the first pot she made wasn't fit for human consumption. The second pot was just slightly better.

"Let me try this time," her grandmother said, elbowing her aside.

Still bleary eyed from lack of sleep, Madison didn't object. She sank into a kitchen chair and rested her eyes while Granny Bert tried her luck with the coffee maker.

It seemed only seconds later when her grandmother set a mug of brewed coffee in front of her. "Try this," she said.

"Better," Madison agreed. "I hereby appoint you as the official coffeemaker for this trip."

Granny Bert snorted. "You probably made it weak on purpose, just to hornswoggle me into doing the job."

With an enigmatic smile half-hidden behind the rim of the mug, Madison reminded her, "I learned from the best."

Oddly enough, the older woman seemed pleased with her comment.

Pouring a second cup for herself, her grandmother asked what was in the packet Dom left.

"I don't know yet," Madison said. "Brash and I agreed to open it this morning, when our minds were fresh."

"Good luck with that," Granny Bert muttered. "Who knew we'd get only a few hours' sleep last night? I can't believe Miss Wanda and Miss Sybil slept through that sound."

"Does Brash have any theories?"

Madison lifted a slim shoulder. "He says cougars sound like a woman screaming. Maybe that's what it was."

Granny Bert's gray head bobbed in agreement. "Could have been. I've heard that chilling sound before. It will make the hairs on your neck stand on end."

Madison nibbled her bottom lip. "It certainly sounded close."

"So, no wandering around after dark," her grandmother noted.

"Maybe Dom knew there were cougars and mountain lions here. Maybe that was part of his reluctance to come."

"He could buy a gun to ward them off for a lot less than he's paying you."

"There's still those thirteens to consider," Madison mumbled, taking another sip of the strong brew. "The man is definitely superstitious." After several more sips, her brain woke up, and she thought to ask, "By the way. Did it strike you as windy last night?"

"I didn't hear it blowing if that's what you mean. And from what little I could see when I peeked out the windows, it didn't look so."

"Hmm. I didn't think so, either, but the trees on that far ridge were certainly swaying."

"Trees? Normally, the tops of the mesas are as flat as Myrna Lewis' chest."

Myrna Lewis was one of Madison's few nemeses in The Sisters. Shaking the unwanted image of the shapeless woman and her total lack of fashion sense from her mind, Madison insisted, "I definitely saw trees on top of the plateau. If not trees, at least saplings or tall grass. It was steadily swaying to the right, so I assume it was windier up there than it was down here."

"I still say the mesas are flat. Too many rocks and boulders up there for trees to grow."

"So maybe it wasn't the caprock. Maybe it's just a very high hill with trees."

"Not likely," her grandmother snorted. "Go look out the window and see for yourself."

Unable to resist the taunt, Madison shoved from her chair and marched to the window above the sink. She pushed the curtain aside and craned her neck to see the top of the ridge in the distance.

"Well? How many trees do you see up there?" her grandmother wanted to know.

With a thoughtful frown, Madison admitted, "Not nearly enough to explain what I saw last night."

5

Brash appeared in the kitchen less than twenty minutes later.

"What happened to you sleeping for another hour?" Madison asked with a worried expression upon her face. "You must be exhausted."

"Am," he acknowledged gruffly, heading straight to the coffee pot. "But I can't sleep. Not until I know what's inside this packet," he waved the manila envelope in his hand, "and what the hell that noise was last night."

"Maddy said you thought it was a cougar." Granny Bert's voice was sharp as she tossed her granddaughter an accusing look.

His only reply was an unintelligible grunt.

Joining the women, Brash tossed the envelope onto the table and pulled up a chair. "Maddy, see exactly what this mission entails."

Madison pulled a thick sheaf of papers from the packet. She thumbed through them quickly, confused by the contents within. "Uhm, this looks like a will of some sort. Phillip Perkins, dated ... over forty years ago." There was a question in her voice as she read the date.

"That was their granddaddy."

Virgie's voice startled them all as she came into the kitchen. "Dom and Robert's. He started the ranch and left it to his seven sons when he died."

"But why leave me a copy? Isn't that rather personal?" Madison wondered aloud.

"My guess," Brash said, "is there's some clause in there that will explain its purpose for being included in the packet. May I?" he asked, reaching for the document.

"Of course." She handed it over before scanning through the remaining papers. "Here's a rough sketch of the ranch's layout. A list of names with notations or question marks beside each. Apparently, Norman Perkins is the foreman of sorts. Terrance Perkins acts as CEO and general manager. He's not sure who or what role Ricardo Reyes plays." She shuffled through more papers. "There's a list of telephone numbers we may need. And a list of..." her brow knotted with confusion "people we can trust. There are exactly two names on the list. This second list, however, is full of people we may or may not be able to trust."

"What in the world?" Virgie murmured. "What has Dom gotten us involved in?"

"From the looks of this last list, I would say some kind of family feud. Half the names on the questionable list are Perkins."

"That sounds about like Dom!" Virgie huffed.

"Then why did you bring us all out here?"

Granny Bert demanded.

"It sounded like a good idea at the time," Virgie defended herself. "A week away from the grind of everyday life and a chance to see the ranch one last time. A nice, fat paycheck for Maddy didn't hurt none, either."

Ignoring the two women across from her, Madison looked through the remaining papers. "These are the instructions for what he wants from me. There are a few more on here than mentioned over the phone." Without raising her head, she gave Miss Virgie a stern, disapproving look before continuing, "Must stay seven days, seven nights. Must remain on the property, yada, yada, yada, no matter what I see or hear. Which, now, of course," she muttered, "I understand."

Returning to the list, she continued to read, "Can't bring a black cat. But this is the new part. Must determine if there is a threat to my—meaning Dom's— life. If yes, must have proof of accusation. A list of suspects would be nice." She stared up at Miss Virgie. "Are you kidding me? Did you know about this?"

"Of course not! I told you exactly what Dom told me. He suspected something was going on out here, but he didn't know what. He wanted you to sniff out what it might be."

"He never mentioned that his life could be at stake?"

"Absolutely not! Not in so many words, at least."

Granny Bert turned to her old friend. Perhaps

it was because she had known her for so long. Perhaps it was because Virgie had married a man who was raised alongside Bertha and her brothers, making her almost like family. Or perhaps it was because the two women were so much alike.

"How few words did he use?" Granny Bert asked suspiciously. "What aren't you telling us?"

"There was some nonsense about local legend and a curse, but I'm sure that was all it was. Nonsense."

"What curse, Miss Virgie?" Madison's voice came out stern and glinting, much like the expression in her hazel eyes.

"Something about being the thirteenth heir."

"And you just now thought to mention this?"

"I told you there was the run of the mill ghost story or two. Campfire tales. Urban legends." She made a fluttering motion with her hand. "Whatever they're calling foolish and baseless superstitions these days."

"Campfire tales and supposed curses are one thing. Not many people call those a death threat," Madison pointed out.

"I told you, Dom is a wuss. Someone mailed him an old newspaper article. He ran into a string of bad luck. He made it into something bigger than it is. I told you, he likes to exaggerate."

"Maybe not," Brash's deep voice broke in. "There's a clause in the will. Old man Perkins left the ranch to his seven sons, and it can only be passed to male descendants. I'll save you the therefores and whereas-es but from what I can determine, if one of the heirs fails to claim his share of the estate for any reason, ownership becomes capped at the first twelve heirs to—and I quote— 'avoid hostilities and grievances among the family.' Apparently, Dom is heir number thirteen. My guess," he told the women, "is that someone wants to keep him from claiming his fair share of the family legacy."

"But to threaten his life?" Granny Bert asked. "That's cold. Particularly for family members."

"If they know how superstitious he is, they don't need to make a direct threat. They can use his own fears against him to scare him off."

"If that's the case, where do I come in?" Madison asked. "How can I prove or disprove that someone is out to get him, whether it be psychologically or physically?"

Brash heaved a sigh. "I'm not sure, but we have seven days to figure it out."

"Look on the bright side," Virgie said. "Since he's already paid half the money upfront, the most you have to lose is the other half."

"But if the threat is physical," Madison pointed out, "Dom could lose his life."

Her comment set a somber mood at the table, until Miss Sybil sauntered into the room with a bright smile upon her face.

"Good morning, roomies! And how are we this morning? I don't know about y'all, but I slept like a baby last night."

As she turned her back to pour the last of the coffee, Granny Bert muttered, "You're right. Last night, I slept about like I did when Joe Bert was a baby. He was a terrible sleeper, that one."

"Shall I put on another pot?" Miss Sybil asked.

She was taken aback by the overeager 'yeses' shouted her way. Her dark eyes batted in concern as tears threatened. She thought she had said or done something wrong.

Hoping to soften their sleep-deprived responses, Madison offered, "Granny Bert has been appointed our official barista. She'll help."

While lumbering to her feet, Granny Bert 'accidentally' kicked her granddaughter beneath the table. Her apology dripped with sarcasm, but she didn't complain as she went to help her best friend.

To the two left at the table, Brash said, "Miss Virgie, I thought you might like to go with me today while I explore the ranch."

"I'd love to!"

"What about me?" Madison asked, trying not to feel slighted.

"There's the others to consider," he said, telegraphing a silent message through his dark gaze. He needed her there to protect their elder housemates, even though he would never say as much to Granny Bert's face. "Besides, Miss Virgie is the only one even remotely familiar with the ranch and the people here. They may be more willing to talk to her than they are to me."

"I suppose you're right," Madison agreed with reluctance. "And someone has to stay here at all times, so I may as well take my turn."

"By the way, was there anything in that will to make that stipulation necessary?" Virgie wanted to know.

"Not that I saw. I think it must be another of Dom's quirks."

"That, or a safety precaution," Madison reasoned. "Once people know he's here to claim his inheritance, they may try to harm him."

"Are you trying to make me feel guilty for not taking you?" Brash frowned.

"Of course not. But it's a reasonable assumption. Maybe guarding the house 24/7 is his way of making certain there's no surprises in store."

The frown persisted. "I'm not sure of the logic. Dom isn't the one here, so it's a moot point, don't you think?"

"Only if the one trying to frighten him away doesn't realize he sent someone in his stead. Unless they've had eyes on us since we arrived, they may think he's here with us."

"Maybe I shouldn't go out, after all."

"Don't be ridiculous. We didn't come all this way to be holed up in the house the entire time."

"But I'd be leaving you defenseless."

Overhearing his words as she returned to the table, Granny Bert demanded, "Who are you calling defenseless? I've been handling a gun since before you were born, sonny. And so has Sybil. Don't think for one minute that we can't hold our own with a shotgun, rifle, *or* a pistol!"

"Wanda's no slouch in the shooting department, either," Miss Sybil added, close on her friend's heels. "Don't forget she chased her cheating husband and Pearl Simpson out of her house with a shotgun. She only missed their naked behinds because she intended to."

"As long as we keep her away from the margaritas and her medicinal marijuana, she's a cracker-jack shot," Granny Bert confirmed.

The woman in question popped up in the doorway, a big smile on her face. "Are y'all talking about me? Oooh, let me guess! We're going to have a shooting contest while we're here, aren't we? I put twenty on myself."

"No shooting competition, I'm afraid," Brash said. "But it's good to know you're all comfortable with a gun. No telling what kind of varmints there are out here in this rough terrain." He played it off as nothing more than a matter of man vs. nature. Or, in this case, woman vs. nature.

"No worries there. I can shoot at weasels with four legs as easily as I can at those with two." Miss Wanda rubbed her hands together and surveyed the cold burners of the stove. "Who wants eggs and pan toast for breakfast? I'll cook," she offered.

Madison leaned over to her husband with a wink. "See? If nothing else, Miss Wanda will keep things lively. Her talents don't stop with a gun, you know. She does her best work with a spatula and a frying pan. And her cakes are almost as good as Genny's."

He crooked a skeptic brow. "So, if nothing else, we'll be well-fed on this adventure."

Even though the other women moved toward the stove to help cook, Madison lowered her voice to ask, "Are you sure about going out today?"

"Like you said, we can't stay holed up in here the entire time. While breakfast is cooking, I'll look around the yard. After that, we can venture further out. We'll go up to the main house and introduce ourselves."

"You're good with taking Miss Virgie?"

"If you mean do I wish I could take you instead, of course I do. I always want you near me, especially when danger is near. But this isn't just about us this time. And I *do* think having Miss Virgie there will give me an advantage."

"I trust your judgment, sweetheart. And I understand. I'll be fine here at the house. If I can get the Wi-Fi to work, I'll dig around and see what I can find on local legends and such."

"Sounds good." He drained his cup and stood. "I'll take a stroll around the house and make certain everything's secure. I shouldn't be long."

"Should I come with you?"

He hesitated only a second too long. "If you'd like." At her raised brow, he explained, "I just want to be sure everything's on the up and up. I'd feel better if you stayed here. I won't be long, I promise."

"Be. Careful." She punctuated each word with a poke into his flat stomach.

He gave her an easy smile. "Always."

With the sketch of the ranch in hand, after breakfast, Brash and Virgie headed out toward the ranch's main house. Brash insisted it was good manners to alert their presence to those in charge.

How else, he reasoned, could they know their group had permission to be there and weren't simply trespassing on private land? Before leaving, however, he pressed a hard kiss onto her lips and an urgent warning into her ear.

"Keep your guns with you at all times. No matter what, do not go outside that door or let anyone inside. At this point, we still don't know what we're dealing with. With any luck, it's nothing more than Dom's superstitious worries, and we're grossly over-prepared, but I'm not taking any chances. Not with your and their safety on the line."

"And yours," she was quick to remind him.

"Right. If you need me and can't get me on the cell, use the satellite phone. Again, probably overkill, but I believe in taking all the proper precautions."

Madison felt better knowing their communication didn't depend on unreliable cell phone coverage. Already, her hopes for a good Wi-Fi connection were as weak as the flickering signal itself.

"Good luck. Love you," she said as she gave him another kiss.

"Love you, too. We'll try to hurry."

With the two of them gone and the house locked and secure, Wanda wandered into the kitchen to see if she had the makings for a cake. Miss Sybil gravitated toward the bookcase in the living room, while Madison pulled out her laptop and tried in vain to find a Wi-Fi signal. Granny Bert took the position of sentry, circling the perimeter of the house's interior with the Glock in her pocket and the shotgun in her arms.

When she came back from one round looking tired and sweaty, Madison grew suspicious.

"What's wrong?" she asked, sidling up to her grandmother so not to worry their companions.

"Nothing."

"Then why do you sound like you're half out of breath?"

"Because I am! It's hard work moving furniture."

"Why were you moving furniture?"

"Just securing the back door. If someone else has the key, and they want in badly enough, a heavy chest of drawers should at least slow them down long enough for us to get off a few shots."

"You should have called for help."

"Nah, I got it just fine. It's good to use the old muscles now and then."

Madison shot a worried glance toward the front door. "And that one?"

Granny Bert flashed a smile. "Has a key to get in, an inside chain, a deadbolt without a key, and four women with guns."

"Good point."

"I'll take a five-minute breather and then make another round."

"I'll make rounds this time." Seeing the objection form on her grandmother's lips, she hastily added, "I need the exercise, especially if Miss Wanda is baking a cake." Granny Bert wouldn't appreciate knowing that her physical exertion was so easy to spot.

"Fine, fine. But I have the next round. You can't have all the cake for yourself, you know."

Hiding a grin, Madison agreed to the conditions. "Absolutely."

6

Naomi and Juliet, Texas
Otherwise known as "The Sisters"

The Sisters Independent School District was closed for the day due to a water leak. With some of the classrooms flooded and the water main turned off, there was no choice but to keep students away.

Bethani had plans to sleep away the unexpected windfall, while Blake asked to accompany his step-grandfather with ranch chores. Over a hardy breakfast, Andrew deCordova told the teen he was pleased to have him. If they finished early, there might be time to wet a hook and line.

Bethani's lazy day came to an abrupt halt with one phone call.

"Bethani? It's Aunt Genny. I hear you have the day off from school, and I desperately need your help."

Genetically, Genesis Montgomery wasn't her aunt, but she was family in all the ways that mattered. As Madison's best and oldest friend, she had been there for all the major events in Bethani's life. Best of all, she had been there for many of the everyday moments, as well. Bethani knew she could always depend on her 'aunt.' In turn, Bethani would do anything for Genny, even if it meant giving up her bonus day off.

Without asking for details, Bethani ran a hand through her tousled blond hair—she and her twin claimed they got their blond hair and blue eyes from Genny—and replied, "Sure. Whatcha need? Do you need help with the girls?"

"Hope has a runny nose, and I'm taking her to the doctor."

"Do I need to come over and watch Faith?"

Hope and Faith were Genny and Cutter's 'almost' twins. After Genny and Madison stumbled across an adoption scam, and fearful they couldn't have children of their own, the Montgomerys agreed to adopt an expectant mother's unborn child. Soon after, they discovered Genny was pregnant. Dark-haired Hope was born less than six weeks before the fair-complexioned Faith. Now the restaurateur had her hands full, trying to juggle two newborns and the most popular eatery in The Sisters.

"Actually, Megan said she could come. Is there any way you can work a shift at *New Beginnings*? Two people called in today. One is sick, the other has three kids at home now, thanks to the water leak."

"Sure. Let me get ready, and I'll be there as soon as I can."

"You're a lifesaver! Thanks, Beth. Love you!"

"Love you, too. And I hope little Hope is okay."

"I'm sure it's nothing, but if she gets sick, so

will Faith. I remember how you and Blake shared sore throats and coughs when you were little."

"And chicken pox," Bethani said dryly. "I still haven't forgiven him for this nice little scar one of the sores left above my eyebrow." She rubbed the tiny blemish in question, so minute no one but she was aware of its existence.

"Sibling love," Genny quipped. "You gotta love it."

"I suppose," the eighteen-year-old grumbled. "Let me know what the doctor says about Hope. Be safe."

Bethani hurried through her morning routine, securing her long, blond hair into a ponytail and foregoing most of her makeup. Even though her complexion was fair, her skin was smooth and unblemished, needing little in the way of enhancement. A touch of lip gloss and a dab of blush, and she was good.

When the babies were born, she and her stepsister had eagerly promised to help Genny whenever needed. Megan had experience with a younger sibling (a half-brother when her mom remarried), but Bethani hadn't been around many infants before. She loved her 'cousins' dearly and was happy to hold and cuddle them, but their cries left her feeling helpless and inept. It seemed only natural for Megan to carry most of the babysitting duties, while Bethani found other ways to help. She didn't mind washing and folding their adorable outfits, and, quite by accident, she had found herself helping at the café a few times. Genny insisted on paying both girls a weekly salary, so the arrangement worked well for all of them.

Bethani shot off a text to her mother informing her of the change in plans, updated her step-grandmother, hugged her goodbye, and arrived at *New Beginnings Café* in time for the breakfast rush.

"Thank the good Lord you're here!" Thelma greeted her. The middle-aged woman had been with Genny since day one and had seen business blossom to the point of near bursting. "Can you take that far table? They've been waiting several minutes, but there's only two of us and all of them." She motioned to the one other waitress working. Every table, booth, and bar stool were currently occupied.

"No problem."

Bethani looped the apron with the *New Beginnings* logo over her neck, secured it around her slim waist, grabbed three menus, and headed to the back table. The buoyant smile on her face bobbed and faltered when she saw the woman seated there.

Of all people, her first customer of the day had to be Myrna Lewis! It seemed an omen of sorts, setting an ominous tone for the day. Mrs. Lewis had disliked Bethani and her mother since the day they had moved there. Or at least since the day Bethani had videoed one of her many outrageous outbursts and called her out on a lie, right here in this very restaurant. It had taken more courage than she thought she possessed at the time (fifteen, new in town, and still raw and reeling from her father's sudden death), but she couldn't sit by and let that obnoxious woman tell lies about innocent kids she vaguely knew from school. Even with their hokey country-bumpkin names like Buddy Ray and Jimmie Kate, they didn't deserve to be brushed aside like the flowers she claimed their steer had trampled and their goat had eaten. Their little sister, the one that woman had chased with a broom, certainly hadn't deserved such treatment! Bethani was compelled to stand up for them, even when it meant standing up to the devil, herself.

Nonetheless, she tucked away her personal grievances and gave the trio a chirpy greeting. "Good morning! Welcome to *New Beginnings*. To start your day, can I get you some coffee or something to drink?"

"You can give us our menus!" Myrna snapped. She snatched the middle menu from Bethani's hands, causing the others to spill onto the table. It was her fault, but she blamed the girl. "Look at how clumsy you are! Do you know we have been sitting here for eight and one-half minutes? Not a single waitress has been by to greet us or offer us service. Where is that Genesis Baker? I want to lodge a complaint."

To herself, Bethani thought, *I bet you do. It's like your favorite past-time.*

Aloud, she said, "I'm sorry. Genesis *Montgomery* is off today. I'm sorry no one has been over yet, but as you can see, we're rather busy. But I'm here now and happy to serve you." She directed her smile to the couple seated across from the grumpy woman. "Would you care for a cup of coffee?

It's our own special blend."

"That sounds lovely," the woman smiled. She was dressed in a business suit and pearls and looked completely out of place here in the small towns of Naomi and Juliet. Bethani wondered if she were some sort of lawyer. "With cream, please."

"I'll have a cup, black," her male companion said. He wore a suit and tie.

Across from them, Myrna wore her customary mishmash of patterns and colors. Bethani resisted the urge to roll her eyes at the sight of her yellow t-shirt, bright orange sweater, orangy-pink plaid knee-length shorts, and her black man-socks paired with white sneakers. The round, shapeless woman had even less fashion sense than Mom did!

Bethani had to admit, however, that her mother's wardrobe had improved since Daddy D and Derron came into her life. She often forgot that her mother's employee, with his impeccable wardrobe and stylish hair, was the nephew of the orange blob seated at the booth.

"I'll have a cup, too," Myrna said. "Make sure the coffee's hot."

"I'll be right back with the coffee and to take your order," Bethani promised.

As she turned away, she heard Mrs. Lewis' nasal whine. "You can see how poorly managed the place is. There's definitely room for another restaurant here in town. A place that knows about *true* service."

Bethani returned just minutes later, carrying three empty mugs, a small pitcher of cold cream, and a thermos of hot, steaming coffee. She deposited them with care and proceeded to fill the mugs with the hot, fragrant brew.

"Have you decided what you'd like for breakfast?"

"Oh, are you still serving breakfast?" Myrna asked in an overly innocent voice, her meaning clear. "I thought you might have moved on to the noon menu, as late as it is."

Bethani's smile never faltered. "No, ma'am, we're still serving Miss Genny's special recipe French toast and cheesy grits, along with the regular menu favorites. What sounds good today?"

"So... what?" Myrna persisted, determined to dampen the girl's day. "Is Genny so understaffed that she pulled you out of school to come down and work? Aren't there laws against child labor and skipping school?"

"Gee," Bethani said, her eyes wide with exaggerated innocence and gullibility. "I would imagine so, but I'm eighteen, and there's no school today because of a water leak."

With a disgruntled sniff, Myrna was unrelenting. "Cheeky little thing, aren't you?" she grumbled.

Bethani flashed her a bright smile. "They say I get my dimples from Aunt Genny!"

"Why, of all foolishness! You aren't even related. I've never heard such malarkey." She shifted her ample behind on the chair and propped her elbows on the table, eyes glaring at the menu. "As if you can *choose* your relatives at will!"

"You know," Bethani said thoughtfully, "I often hear Derron say those exact words." She turned her smile to the other couple while Myrna sputtered with outrage. "Have you two decided, or do you need more time?"

"No, the French toast sounds delicious," the stylish woman replied.

"Would you prefer bacon, sausage, or ham with that?"

"Do you have turkey bacon?" the woman asked with doubtful hope.

"Of course. It also comes with fresh fruit. Would you like anything else?"

"No, that sounds like more than enough."

Beside her, the man placed his order. "I'll have the cheesy grits. It has bacon in it?"

"Yes, sir," Bethani said, jotting it down on her pad. "It also comes with a side of bacon, ham, or sausage. Which would you care for?"

"Bacon, bacon, bacon," he jested.

"Absolutely. You'll also get buttermilk biscuits and fresh fruit. Or, if you prefer, toast."

"Biscuits, please."

During her brief stint as a waitress, Bethani had already picked up the qualities of a good server. With a conspiratorial wink, she confided, "Good choice. They're homemade." She hid her dread as she turned to the third customer. "And you, Mrs. Lewis? What would you like today?"

"A proper waitress!"

"I think she's been delightful," the suited woman interjected.

Myrna gave another sniff. "I suppose she's learning. I'll have an order of two eggs, over easy. No hard middle, but not oozing yellow, either. No broken yolks."

Bethani took note of her demands. "Would you like hash browns or country-style potatoes with that?"

"Does the country-style have onions?"

"Yes, ma'am, along with peppers and a touch of chorizo sausage. Not hot, but spicy."

"Then, no. I'll have the regular hash browns."

"Biscuits or toast?"

"Toast. One white and one wheat."

"Very well. Anything else?"

"Does mine include fruit?"

"Yes, ma'am."

"What kind?"

"I believe it's a mix of seasonal fruit."

"Make certain it's ripe, and not half-green. Quality hothouse fruit is so hard to come by."

"I'll ask the kitchen to make certain your fruit is fully ripened." It was all Bethani could do to keep from clenching her teeth. "Will there be anything else before I go?"

Myrna took a noisy slurp of coffee. "This is tepid!" she complained.

"I'll bring a fresh cup."

"Miss?" a man at the next table called.

"Be right there," Bethani promised over her shoulder. She tried wrapping up business at Myrna's table. "If that's all, I'll put your order in and bring you that new cup."

"What if I'm not through ordering?"

"I'm sorry. What else would you like, Mrs. Lewis?"

"Nothing. But you're so eager to run off to that other table, you simply cut us short."

Refusing to bow to the other woman's rudeness, Bethani neither groveled nor argued. "I didn't mean to give that impression," she replied calmly.

The man behind them was turning impatient, even though Bethani wasn't his server. "Miss? Can we get the check?"

"Well?" Myrna demanded. "Are you going to keep him waiting like you did us? Do your job, girl!"

The entire meal followed a similar pattern. No matter what Bethani did, Myrna complained. The steaming coffee was, according to her, only lukewarm. One of her egg yolks was busted (Bethani suspected she poked it with a fork, as it had come out of the kitchen fully intact), the toast was too crispy and dry, and the fruit was soggy and overripe. When she rolled out of her chair and waddled out of the restaurant, she left a paltry quarter beside her plate.

In contrast, the couple across the table from her raved about their meal. The man cleaned his plate, the woman protested the portions were too huge to finish, and a twenty-dollar bill snugged beneath a coffee cup when they left, along with a handwritten note.

In a flourishing hand, the woman had written: *You've been an excellent server. I would love to have you work for me in one of my restaurants. I offer a very generous salary.*

She had underlined very two times and included her name and phone number.

Pleased with the compliment, Bethani tucked the note into her pocket along with the twenty-dollar and twenty-five cent tip.

Perhaps her day wasn't ruined, after all.

7

Miss Sybil called her name as Madison stubbornly tried to get a Wi-Fi connection of some sort. Even after an hour or more of trying, she had no luck.

"Maddy, dear?"

She could use the distraction. Standing and stretching, she turned her attention to the older woman. "Yes, ma'am?"

"I think I found something you might want to see. These are old scrapbooks. Mostly they're newspaper clippings from the local paper. Like ours, their paper only comes out once a week, and most are from years past. But there's still plenty to read in here."

"Of course," Madison murmured. "Old school. Why didn't I think of that?"

"See these? There's a story about some local legend. Supposedly, it happened right here, on this ranch."

"Can I see that?" she asked eagerly.

Miss Sybil handed over the bulky book.

"That's why I called you. See for yourself."

Madison thumbed through the book before settling on a page to read. "This looks like a series of articles, one published each week in the month of October," Madison noted. "The first one is about the legend of *La Llorona*."

Granny Bert nodded. "I've heard of her. She's very prominent in Hispanic culture. Translated, it means 'the weeping woman.' It's the tale of a woman who has been betrayed by the father of her children. In a fit of madness and despair, she drowns her children to punish the husband. When she comes to her senses and realizes what she's done, she throws herself into the water to kill herself. Now, her spirit roams the river and creek beds, forever searching for her children."

"That's a horrible story!" Madison protested.

Her grandmother shrugged. "I didn't make it up, just telling you the legend."

Still frowning, Madison scanned the article, dismayed to find that it closely followed Granny Bert's rendition.

"According to this, it's believed that she has been spotted here on the ranch numerous times over the years. She walks along the mountain ridges and along the river bank, dressed all in white, searching for her children." She read a few more paragraphs before inhaling a sharp gasp.

"What? What does it say?" Granny Bert asked.

"I know it's just a legend. But it says here that she cries continuously, wailing and keening until it escalates into a chilling, blood-curdling scream in the night."

"Like we heard last night?" her grandmother asked.

"What?" asked Miss Sybil. "What did we hear last night?"

"Those of us not sleeping on our good ear heard exactly that. A chilling, blood-curdling scream."

"Why didn't you wake me?" her friend cried.

"I figured if you could sleep through that, you deserved the peace and quiet. Let me tell you. That was as awful a sound as I ever did hear."

Enthralled, Sybil asked in a hushed voice, "What did you do? Did everyone hear it?"

"Everyone but you and Wanda. The rest of us made a sweep through the house, making certain the doors and windows were locked. Brash sat up the rest of the night at the top of the stairs, a gun in his lap. I spelled him at dawn."

"Is that what this is all about?" Sybil asked, imitating walking back and forth with her fingers. "Circling the house like some sort of guard on duty?"

"In a manner of speaking."

"Speak a little plainer," Sybil told her long-time friend.

Granny Bert released a weary sigh. "We may as well call Wanda in here and get it over with, so that everyone is on the same page."

With the situation explained, the working theory of Dom being the thirteenth heir and the use of superstitions and local lore to scare him away, Sybil and Wanda were left with similar reactions for different reasons.

"I don't hold with no haints," Miss Sybil said, using the old way of saying 'haunts.' Her thin shoulders shivered with apprehension.

In direct contrast, Wanda's large berth shimmied with intrigue. "Oooh, I love a good ghost story! Count me in!"

"I'm not sure it's a matter of being in or out," Madison protested. "I'm just telling you what we suspect and what this article says."

"If you hear the screaming lady again, be sure and wake me up! I'd love to hear that."

"Ooo-kay. Moving on," Madison said, turning a page in the scrapbook. "This article came out the next week, recounting the legend of *lechuza*. A *lechuza*, which is Spanish for owl, is basically a barn owl. Mexican folklore has it that *la lechuza* is a witch who sold her soul to the devil for magical powers. Others believe it's the spirit of a woman who has been murdered. Either way, the beast has a bird-like body with a woman's face. When *la lechuza* hunts at night, or some believe that if you even hear the shapeshifting witch's cry—which, interestingly enough, sounds like a long, harsh scream— it's an omen that someone in your family will die."

"What's with all the Mexican ghosts?" Wanda wanted to know. "Did we cross the border and someone forget to tell me? Because if we did, I need to find some Mexican vanilla and some good quality tequila."

"Hold your britches," Granny Bert warned. "We're still in Texas. Not all that far from the border but still in Texas."

"Oh, poo." Wanda put her hands on her ample hips and huffed her disappointment. "I could use a good, stiff margarita about now. Nothing like a 'rita with a ghost story."

"Go check your cake. I think I smell it burning."

"Hold your place in that book," Wanda instructed Madison. "I'll be back before you can jump out and say 'boo!'"

Watching her hurry from the room, Madison snickered, "She really does like her ghost stories, doesn't she?"

"She may, but I don't!" Miss Sybil wailed. "No one told me there would be haints out here!"

"There's no such thing as haints," Granny Bert said in rebuke. "Or ghosts, as they're called in the twenty-first century."

"Then how do you explain all that stuff in the newspaper?"

"It's nothing but legend. Long before playpens and house alarms were invented, Mexican mothers would tell the tale of *La Llorona* to keep their kids from wandering around in the dark."

"That was cruel."

"Cruel but effective. Better to have kids drown in a made-up story than in real life."

"True enough," Miss Sybil agreed.

Wanda came back in, her face flushed. "I'm back. You can go ahead now."

"The next week highlighted some of the rumors of bad luck surrounding the number thirteen." Looking down at the scrapbook, Madison read the article aloud, "The number thirteen has long been condemned as unlucky. People who truly fear the number are called triskaidekaphobics. They believe it's unlucky to have thirteen guests at a dinner party, a thirteenth floor on a high-rise building, or to marry or do any form of important business on a day with this dreadful date. Why, you may ask?

"Reasons include the fact there were thirteen people at the Last Supper, and that Judas, the one to betray Jesus, was the thirteenth guest to arrive. A witches' coven originally had thirteen members, and tradition says there were thirteen steps leading up to the gallows. Triskaidekaphobics believe that people with thirteen letters in their name are cursed. Examples include Charles Manson, Jack the Ripper, Jeffrey Dahmer, Theodore Bundy, and Adolfus Hitler, who was most commonly known as Adolf. Last but in no way the least, in many schools of numerology, twelve is considered the perfect number. It represents completion. Therefore, the addition of just one more number is somehow wrong. If twelve is perfection, thirteen must be unlucky."

"I like the number thirteen," Wanda said, oddly offended by the article. "I once won thirteen hundred dollars on nickels, playing a Lucky 13 slot machine. You remember that, Sybil. Don't you?"

"I think that was the trip when I had thirteen margaritas and wiped my memory clean," the other woman bemoaned.

"Are there any other articles in there that

might help?" Granny Bert wanted to know.

"These were all published a few years ago in the month of October, so there was one more just before Halloween. It's a local tale of what some call the Perkins Curse. According to this, on October 13, 2013, there were reports of a huge ruckus that took place at the ranch." Madison read the words straight from the newsprint. "Strange lights flashed and crisscrossed the night sky. A vicious wind came up, swirling and twisting, louder than a locomotive. Believing a sudden twister was brewing, Terrance Perkins instructed employee Geraldo Reyes to check out the area, making certain no livestock were in danger. Reyes was last seen approaching the ridge in a company pickup. When the winds settled, and the lights went dim, there was no sign of Reyes or the truck. Neither were ever seen again."

As she read the article, the women around her gasped.

Eyes wide, Miss Wanda whispered in horrified fascination, "They disappeared?"

Madison gave a half shrug, half nod. "I suppose. This says that strangely enough, the skies over the rest of the ranch were clear. The sudden whirlwind was contained to the immediate area along Mount Perkins known as Perkins Ridge, and meteorologists confirmed there was no tornado that night." She scanned through the next paragraph. "Most people believe it was the work of *La Llorona*. They believe Reyes' interference made the ghost angry and she put a curse on not only him, but the entire ranch. Almost immediately, there were reports of strange happenings. People believed it was proof *La Llorona* had hexed the ranch. The bad luck could only be attributed to the curse, they claimed."

Granny Bert was skeptical. "What kind of happenings?"

Madison looked back at the article, her finger running along the black typeface. "Lightning struck a tree and killed seven of the ranch's best heifers as they rested beneath it. A cowboy fell off his horse and into a den of rattlesnakes. A stock pond turned over, its water suddenly bad." Her lip crinkled with a disapproving smirk. "There's more examples, all of them nothing more than conjecture and coincidence. But it was enough to convince people there *was* such a thing as the Perkins Curse."

"Utter foolishness," her grandmother huffed.

"Does any of that help us with our situation?" Miss Sybil asked.

"I think maybe it does." Madison's face took on a thoughtful expression. "Think about it. If Dom Hebert is as superstitious as Miss Virgie says, they could use all of this to play tricks on his psyche. The house number alone is enough to spook him. If his real name is Dominic, that's thirteen letters, and he's already convinced he's cursed. Tales of owl sightings or an occasional *la lechuza* would be interpreted as an omen of death. Mention of *La Llorona* would probably keep him from wandering around in the dark, just as the story was intended for children. Plus, throw in the Perkins Curse, and I could definitely see Dom wanting no part of his inheritance and its spooky surroundings."

"If he forfeited," Granny Bert reasoned, "the ranch would be limited to twelve heirs. The perfect number. Or so some believe."

"I'm sure the first twelve heirs do," Madison agreed. "The more I think about it, the more certain I am that that's what this is all about, and what he wanted us to find proof for him."

"It sounds plausible," Miss Sybil agreed, "but how do you prove it?"

"Let's see what, if anything, Brash and Miss Virgie find out before we determine a course of action."

"Bertha, if you spelled Brash at dawn, you're bound to be tired. Why don't you take a nap, and I'll take your place as sentry?" Sybil offered.

"That does sound tempting," Granny Bert admitted. "You'll wake me if something happens?"

"Of course."

"I'll have my Glock at my side. Enter with caution," the old woman warned as she started up the stairs. "No more than an hour, or I'll be spent for the rest of the day."

"I'll wake you myself," Madison promised.

"Wake me sooner if Brash and Virgie return."

An hour and five minutes later, Granny Bert hit the bottom stair step just as the front door jiggled, and Brash's voice called from the other side, "Maddy? It's me. Let us in, sweetheart."

Madison did as asked, relieved to have him

back at the house.

"So? What did you find out?"

"That I need a cup of coffee and a piece of whatever that is I smell coming from the kitchen."

"A basic pound cake," Miss Wanda offered proudly, "with lemon icing, of sorts. I didn't have much to work with."

"Let's go to the kitchen, and we'll fill everyone in," Brash said, his arm firmly around his wife's waist. She noticed that he locked all deadbolts before trailing the older women into the kitchen.

With coffee poured and cake served, they finally shared their findings.

"Only three of the first twelve heirs live on the ranch. A couple of the others have weekend cabins. We met Terrance Perkins, one of the names listed on the questionable side of trust or don't trust. He's the acting CEO of the ranch. He was less than thrilled to know Dom has intentions to claim his inheritance."

"Does he know Dom isn't actually here?" Madison asked. "That he sent us, instead?"

"I avoided the question the best I could, but he was persistent. Wanted Dom—his second cousin from what I can tell— to come up to the house for a visit. I alluded to the fact that Dom got held up in Louisiana but sent us on to get settled."

"How did you explain your connection to Dom?"

"Miss Virgie reminded him she was once married to his cousin and that she had kept up with Dom through the years. As for me, I just said Dom promised to let me hunt."

Miss Virgie shook her head. "Don't let him fool you. Terrance knew exactly who Brash was. He followed his career from college ball to pro, then to his days as a college football coach. He had so many stars in his eyes, he never thought to question your man's connection to Dom. Practically begged him to come hunt over inside the game fence, where he could all but guarantee a trophy kill."

"I guess fame does have its advantages," Madison teased her husband. So far, she hadn't found that to be the case. Then again, her fame came by way of a reality television home renovation show. Brash's began with the legendary sport of football.

A thoughtful frown puckered his forehead. "Actually," Brash said in a slow voice, "I thought it was a bit of overkill. He kept telling me how I *didn't* want to hunt Dom's acreage. Said I wouldn't get a decent shot."

Ever the optimist, Miss Sybil suggested, "Maybe he was trying to be helpful? Do a good deed for his football idol?"

"It's been a long time since I was anyone's idol," Brash objected modestly, "if ever. But it felt like something more than that. And if the property lines on this sketch are to be believed, I saw plenty of wildlife on Dom's side of the fence. That's part of what doesn't add up."

Granny Bert had a thought as she refilled coffee cups. "Don't these hunting outfits usually take pictures with their guests and their harvest? They like to post them on social media and brag about famous people who hunted there, or about what trophy animals they offer. Makes for good publicity. Maybe he wanted you hunting his side for the PR value."

"Could be," Brash agreed. "It just didn't feel that way."

"I reckon he couldn't be too obvious," Virgie pointed out. "Had to come across as sincere."

"I don't know about you, but what came across as sincere to me was his dislike for his cousin. Obviously, there's no love lost between those two."

Virgie nodded. "I got the same impression. Doesn't mean he can't be trusted, though. There's a certain kind of honesty to open hostility. Maybe he just wants to one-up Dom by getting you to endorse his hunting venture."

"It's my understanding that Dom inherits a share of that venture."

"True. But you know how male rivalry works, 'specially among family." Virgie shrugged with a 'whatcha gonna do' expression. "Dom offered his side of the fence, but Terrance offered the whole ranch."

"Did you ask Terrance to set up a visit with Clive Baker, the only person on this ranch listed in the 'trusted' column?" Madison asked.

"Tried, but Terrance was vague about the whole thing. Said Clive was busy on the cattle side of the ranch, culling heifers and steers to be sold."

"By the way," Wanda broke in. "Where did you get the map and the information package y'all keep mentioning? How did it get in the house?"

Virgie had the answer. "Dom said he was

sending the information to the lawyer handling the will. I suppose he saw that it was left here for us to find."

"Makes sense. Anyone want more cake?"

"It was delicious, but I'm good," Brash declared, pushing away his plate.

Having appointed herself as chief cook, Wanda agreed. "When we get hungry, there's makings for a sandwich for lunch. I thought we might try one of the frozen casseroles for dinner. But sometime soon, we'll need to go to the store."

"Maddy, I thought you might like to do the honors," Brash said. "I'll stay here at the house. Granny Bert, you go with her and see what kind of information you can ferret out of the locals," he suggested.

"Good idea," his wife agreed. "While we're gone, Miss Sybil can show you the scrapbook she found. It has some interesting articles from the local paper. I can see where some of the stories could be used against Dom to scare him away."

"Should I go with you? I may remember a landmark or two, in case you get turned around," Virgie offered.

The thought worried Madison. She turned to Brash. "Do you think I might get lost? It was dark last night when we came in. If my GPS doesn't work, I could get turned around."

"The roads were fairly well marked but take a picture of the map with your phone. If you have service now, pull up the directions, screenshot them, and go by those."

Madison bestowed him with a bright smile. "Perfect. Why didn't I think of that?"

"I'm sure you'll find it with no problem. But taking Miss Virgie with you can't hurt."

She was doubtful about leaving him here with Miss Wanda and Miss Sybil for backup but knew Brash could handle any troubles on his own. "It's a plan," she agreed. "I'll grab my purse while y'all double check the list and make certain everything is on it."

Fifteen minutes later, the trio was headed into the tiny town of Manhattan, a dark two-ton pickup with tinted windows following close behind.

8

"I don't know what that guy's problem is, but I wish he'd get off my bumper," Madison grumbled.

"Why don't you slow down and let him go around?" Granny Bert suggested.

"I would if the road would cooperate. There's either a curve or no room to pass."

"It must be someone from the ranch," Virgie observed. "They've been on our tail almost from the minute we turned out of the drive. They should know the road well enough to judge when they can pass." She clucked her tongue in irritation. "I say keep driving and let them deal with the dust."

"I guess I drive slower than they're used to, but I don't know the road." As the front tire found a large pothole and elicited groans all around, Madison muttered, "I give you Exhibit A."

The dark two-ton pickup followed them all the way into the small town of Manhattan. It never tried to pass, never tried to crowd them. Never tried to tap her bumper, even though Madison braced herself, expecting a jolt at any moment. By the time they reached their destination, the muscles in her arms and shoulders were knotted from holding the steering wheel in a death grip.

"It looks even worse in the bright light of day," Granny Bert said, surveying the tiny, dismal town. Against a backdrop of dry, barren dirt dotted with craggy rock formations and prickly grasses, the handful of structures looked tired and worn.

"Grocery store first?" Madison asked. "If they don't have something we need, we can try the only other option, Jackrabbit's."

"I see the truck pulled up at the gas pumps," Granny Bert noted, craning her neck to see through her side mirror. "Don't seem to be getting out. I think they're just parked there to watch us."

"Along with everyone else in town," Madison mumbled. "I feel like there should be banjos playing, like in that movie *Deliverance*."

A dozen or so cars were parked in front of *So-Lo Grocery and Café*, the bulk of them clustered at the far end of the sprawled building. A porch with outdoor seating and a neon sign identified it as the café entrance. Two cars were at the post office, another half dozen trucks at the feed store, and a few others nearer the convenience store portion of the all-purpose enterprise.

The few people inside their vehicles or en route to or from a business stopped what they were doing to stare at the unfamiliar vehicle among them. Madison felt their eyes upon the Expedition as she pulled in at *So-Lo* and parked.

"I thought this was big hunting country out

here," she said. "You'd think they'd be used to unfamiliar vehicles."

"We'd look more the part if we had mud-grip tires and long beards," said Virgie.

"Maybe they recognize us from *Home Again* and think we're doing another reality show," Granny Bert mused. "Say. That's not a bad idea. Maybe we could get a spot on *Rattled*."

Madison shivered with revulsion. "Over my dead body!"

"There you go again," mumbled Virgie, "with your dead body obsession."

"I don't have an obsession. I don't *like* finding dead bodies, particularly my own." Before either of her passengers could speak up, she added testily, "And, no, don't point out that what I just said is impossible."

She made a show of inspecting the town before opening the car door. "I couldn't see well last night, but there's a couple of other buildings on that back street. I see a hair salon and a church."

"Maybe there's hope for this little town yet," Virgie mumbled.

Granny Bert grunted, a sound that could have signaled agreement, could have signaled dispute. "It doesn't look like folks are done with their share of staring yet, so we might as well get this over with and get out."

"I say we split up," Virgie suggested. "Bertha and I can play the part of confused old women, looking for obscure items. Folks like helping little old ladies."

"I wouldn't know," Granny Bert was quick to point out, "being as I'm neither old nor confused, but I'm game for a little play-acting. Virgie, you head to the pharmaceutical section and look for stool softeners. Lord knows Wanda won't need any, but they don't have to know that. I'll find my way over to something in the household section. Big, strong men just love to offer advice on the best mouse trap to use or what pliers are used for." She rolled her eyes with an exaggerated gesture. "They seem to think women are helpless."

"Don't worry about me," Madison said with sarcasm. "I'll be happy to do all the real shopping."

"Don't grumble. You know Virgie and I are better at scooping out dirt."

She couldn't help but agree with her grandmother. "That's true. If anyone can ferret out gossip, it's you two."

"I prefer to call it useful information, thank you very much. Otherwise overlooked and underused tidbits of gold." Granny Bert sniffed.

"Just try to stay out of trouble," Madison warned with a dark glower. She may have slammed the car door a bit harder than necessary.

She ignored the open stares as they made their way into the store. Before going inside, she threw a glance over her shoulder. The dark truck was still at the gas pumps. No one stood beside it to refuel the tank.

The chill creeping down her back told her the occupants sat inside, watching her every move.

Once inside, the three women split up as

planned. Madison took out the list and methodically traveled the aisles, making her selections. Unfamiliar with the store layout, she had to retrace her steps on more than one occasion. It took longer than intended but gave her ample time to conclude that So-Lo was in name only. There was nothing low about the supermarket's prices. She was just thankful that Dom had set up an account for them to use.

She caught a glimpse of her grandmother while searching for the paper goods aisle. Even though the house came stocked with toilet paper, Miss Wanda preferred a different brand. Madison didn't bother greeting her kin, as she was currently busy. Granny Bert looked enthralled with some old rancher's explanation of how to use a toilet plunger. From all the arm motions and hand gestures involved, Madison assumed he offered in-depth instructions.

Biting back a snicker, Madison moved on to the next aisle.

Three aisles over, she found Miss Virgie grilling a store employee about the virtues of which denture paste to use. She was certain Virgie still had her own teeth, but far be it from her to interrupt the woman's choice of extracting information in whatever manner she found useful.

Finally done and standing in line at the register, Madison texted her companions her whereabouts.

While waiting her turn, she sent texts to the twins and Genny, grateful to have a strong signal again. As she read Bethani's message about an eventful day at the café, bits and parts of the conversation in front of her snagged her attention.

"— to his nephew in Louisiana. You know how well that went over. Like a lead-filled balloon! Margaret says Terrance and Norman wanted to protest the will, but there was some clause that forbid it."

"I heard about that," the woman's companion said. "My Billy Ray said the nephew was George's sister's son and hasn't been out here in a long time. Why on earth George would leave the ranch to him is beyond me!"

"George always did have a mind of his own. He was content keeping to himself and not taking part in the hunting side of the business. He liked the cattle and goats better than the wildlife."

"And having only the two girls, he couldn't leave the property to them. I suppose a nephew was his next best choice."

"Still, leaving it to an outsider, and all... Looks like he could have picked one of his cousins who lived around these parts and took an active interest in the ranch."

"I hear the nephew is all kinds of superstitious. If he ever gets wind of all the strange goings-on out there, he may decide not to take his inheritance, after all."

"Isn't that the truth!"

Madison wanted to ask what strange goings-on they referred to, but she knew it was impolite to eavesdrop on other people's conversations. Besides, the women were checking out, and it was now her turn at the checkout stand. As she placed her items onto the conveyor belt, she smiled at the cashier.

"My name is Madison deCordova, and I'm staying at George Perkins' old house. I understand his nephew set up a charge account on my behalf? His name is Dom Hebert."

If she thought people had stared before, it was nothing compared to now. At the mention of the men's names and where she was staying, heads popped up, and conversations came to a halt. Even the women in front of her, now already halfway to the front door, stopped to turn her way.

Madison lifted a hand in a limp wave, offering a wan smile to those around her.

Most of the people turned hastily away, embarrassed, ashamed, or downright guilty of exhibiting bad manners, but a few had no such inhibitions. The cashier was clearly one of the latter.

"Oh, so you know the nephew! I heard an outsider was moving in on us. What's he like? Is he young or old? We could use some fresh meat around here. At my age—I'll be sixty-one on my next birthday—it's getting harder and harder to find a good man."

Madison didn't mention that she had guessed her a decade older. She also didn't mention that she had never met Dom personally.

"I think good men are hard to find at any age," she offered noncommittally. She deftly steered the conversation to another course. "Do you live here in Manhattan?"

The woman nodded as she slid the first item

across the barcode scanner. "About three miles out of town. As you can see, there aren't many houses in the downtown area."

Madison would hardly call the sad collection of random buildings a downtown, but it would be rude to say so. She simply nodded as the woman, whose nametag said Vickie, chattered about the few houses in town. The preacher lived behind the church, a pair of old maid sisters lived in the pink house with the gingerbread trim, a younger couple with five children lived in the house with the old cars parked out front (he was a mechanic, of sorts) and 'a dozen or so others live here and there.' By the time she had rattled off the information, those around them had lost interest in the conversation and gone back to their own business.

Vickie continued ringing up her purchases, until one question created silence once again. "You ain't scared, staying out there at the ranch?" Vickie wanted to know.

Madison darted her eyes around, noting how people anxiously waited to hear her answer. "Scared?"

"Sure, what with all the strange lights and the *La Llorona* sightings. Not to mention the Perkins Curse." She sized Madison up with one head-to-toe perusal. "Say. You ain't staying out there by yourself, are you?"

"No. My husband is with me, as well as... some others." No need to mention that the others were all over the age of eighty. Some—but not Madison, of course— might consider that a weakness.

"Oh. Oh, good. That's good," Vickie said. She sounded genuinely relieved to hear the news. "I'd hate to know you had to face all that alone."

"All what, exactly?" asked Madison.

"Like I said. *La Llorona*. Folks have heard her wails and seen her walking along the hills and riverbed. Throw in the Perkins Curse, and I ain't sure that place is safe to be caught after dark."

Madison heard a few murmurs of agreement from around them. At the checkout beside her, an older man acknowledged, "When I was young and full of piss and vinegar, me and a couple of buddies thought we'd be smart and sneak in there and see it for ourselves. We didn't see nothin', but we heard the cries. Ain't never heard nothing like that before, nor sense. And I've had three wives and raised four daughters! Not a one of them could make that kind of racket."

Vickie and her co-worker were in total agreement.

Madison was about to ask more about the Perkins Curse, but she saw the black pickup truck parked near the doorway, and a hulk of a man coming through the doors. He wore rubber boots caked with mud and worse, unconcerned with the filth he left trailing behind. Snake gaiters covered his boots and jeans up to his knee, and dark sunglasses covered his eyes.

Still, she didn't need to see his eyes to know that he zeroed in on her the moment he walked through the door. They remained on her as he slowly sauntered inside, unzipping his sturdy Carhart jacket as if to say, *Here I am. All six-foot-six inches of me. Anyone care to take me on?*

Once again, the store fell silent. This time, however, Madison felt it was more from fear than it was from curiosity.

Vickie became all thumbs, fumbling through the final items from Madison's cart. Her voice was overly bright when she announced the total due.

"That's going on account, right?" Madison reminded her gently. She didn't understand the woman's sudden clumsiness. Vickie had mentioned being in search of a good man, but instinct told Maddy this wasn't the fluster of an unrequited crush. This had the unmistakable tang of raw fear.

"Right. Oh, yes, that's right," the cashier mumbled, reaching for a clipboard hanging behind the counter.

Madison glanced back toward the doors, but the big man was no longer in sight. Had he gone further into the store or back outside? And where were Granny Bert and Miss Virgie? She felt the need to put eyes on them and know they were all right. As she reached for her phone to text them again, she heard Miss Virgie's voice at the service desk.

"Excuse me, sir. Do you have one of those bells you ring when you get good service? Because, lands sakes alive, you have some of the most helpful salespeople I have ever encountered!"

The manager was clearly pleased to receive such a glowing report. As eyes and attention shifted to the elderly woman gushing her praises at the front desk, Maddy looked around for her grandmother.

She caught sight of her saying goodbye to the older rancher and exchanging what looked like phone numbers. She beckoned for her to hurry.

Done with her enthusiastic review, Virgie joined her friends at the front door, and they all hurried out to the Expedition.

"Don't look now," Madison told the other two women, "but the black truck is parked a few cars down. Load the groceries as quickly as you can and let's get out of here. Something around here doesn't feel right."

"Doesn't sound right, either," Granny Bert grumbled.

Virgie crawled in first. As Madison handed the grocery bags inside, Virgie used little discretion as she piled one upon the other. Granny Bert grabbed the bags with bread and fruit and pulled them with her into the front seat. She barely missed squashing the bananas as she slammed the door behind her.

Normally, Madison would return the shopping cart to its proper place, but she wasn't leaving her companions unattended. She gave it a hearty push, hoping it didn't roll back against her bumper, and quickly started the engine.

Before the big man with the snake gaiters could come barreling out of the store and jump into his own truck, she gunned the accelerator and pulled out onto the highway. She knew he would follow, but it gave her a small sense of control to know she had beat him to the road.

"Text Brash and tell him we're leaving town," she instructed her grandmother. "If he doesn't answer right away, use the satellite phone. I don't want to be out on the road without him knowing when to expect us."

As Granny Bert sent the message, Madison saw the black two-ton truck appear in her rearview mirror. It followed at a steady pace, close enough to be seen but not so close as to pose a threat.

Not an obvious threat, at least.

Still, Madison was immensely relieved when Granny's message went through, and Brash promptly responded.

"He'll be watching for us. We're to use the satellite phone if we have any trouble," Granny Bert relayed.

"Good."

"Want to tell us what in tarnation is going on?"

Madison blew out a deep breath. "Honestly? I have no idea."

"We saw that huge brute of a man come in the store," Miss Virgie said from the backseat, "stomping around like he owned the place. He had his eyes on you like a cougar stalking his prey. Bertha created a little diversion, knocking over a display of paper towels on an end cap. Her friend was nice enough to help her navigate the maze—"

"His name is Hugh," Granny Bert put in.

"—while I dropped a value-sized bottle of aspirins, along with a bottle of peroxide. Those pills scattered and rolled, and when the peroxide hit 'em, they fizzed up like champagne on New Year's Eve! Course, it was right in the path of the big brute, so I hightailed it up to the counter and made a big to-do about the helpful young stocker who offered to clean up my mess. It wasn't much, but it gave us a few minutes to get away."

"You and Granny Bert are so much alike, it's not even funny!" Madison said, laughing in spite of the tension once again building in her shoulders. "How do you two think up these things?"

"Years of practice," her grandmother assured her. "Between the two of us, we had three husbands and six sons. We learned to stay one step ahead of them at all times."

"I feel like such a novice alongside you two."

"Stick with us long enough, kid," Virgie said in her best W. C. Fields' imitation, "and we'll teach you everything we know."

Madison laughed again. "I think that's what Brash is afraid of!" She checked the rearview mirror, finding the black truck still behind them.

No surprise there.

Keeping the Expedition at a steady speed, she told her companions, "I overhead two women talking about the outsider from Louisiana who was inheriting the land, and how Terrance and someone named Norman were none too happy about it. It seems the two men wanted to contest the will, but some clause prohibited it. The women didn't seem to know much about Dom, other than the fact that he's very superstitious. They said if he knew about the strange things that happened at the ranch, he might want no part of it. The cashier made similar remarks, but when the big brute—as you call him— came in, she hushed up and got really nervous."

"He looks like the basic bully," Granny Bert said. "All brawn, no brains."

"He's smart enough to keep two car lengths behind," Madison muttered. "Just close enough to let me know he's following and making no bones about it." She grunted her displeasure before asking, "Did you two find out anything?"

"I found out Hugh is a widower and likes to dance," her grandmother said with a sly smile. "He invited me to the Cattleman's Ball next weekend if I'm still in town."

"You won't be."

"I know that, but he didn't. He was more than happy to tell me all about his little hometown, as long as he thought he might get lucky."

"Granny! What a thing to say!"

"What?" she asked with exaggerated innocence. "I'm a very good dancer. Any man would be lucky to have me for his date to the ball."

"You know good and well— oh, never mind! Just tell me what you found out."

"I found out that everyone around here believes in the so-called Perkins Curse. Out of towners may be eager to come here hunting, but locals don't dare step foot on that ranch for fear of falling victim to the curse. They believe bad luck hangs over the ranch like Spanish moss on an old oak tree. Hugh says they can't keep good hands, because everyone blames every bad thing that ever happens to them on the curse."

"Can you give examples?"

"According to Hugh, there's a ton of them. One

of the ranch hands had a thousand-dollar winning lottery ticket, but a strong gust of wind blew it out of his fingers and swept it into a water puddle, making it illegible."

Rolling her eyes, Madison huffed. "That's hardly a curse."

"The townspeople think it was. One of the housekeepers found a gold watch at the lodge, but before she could turn it in, she was arrested for stealing it. The same week, her dog died, and her husband was bit by a rattlesnake. Not sure if the husband lived or not, but she blamed it all on a full moon and the curse."

"What utter malarkey!"

"I know it, and you know it. Virgie knows it. But the folks in these parts don't seem to. They believe everything comes back to the curse. A drop in cattle prices. A drought. A sudden downpour that destroys crops ready to be harvested. Anybody who lives or works at the ranch who gets a divorce or a bad case of the croup. It all comes back to the curse."

Madison shook her head in amazement. "That's nothing but foolishness."

From the back, Virgie's old eyes twinkled with mirth. "Then how do you explain Bertha knocking over that display, and me making such a mess right in front of that big man?" She shrugged her shoulders and turned up her palms. "We're staying at the ranch. It goes without saying. It must be the Perkins Curse working on us, too."

9

The truck trailed Madison's Expedition back to the ranch, holding at a steady pace behind her. If she slowed down, it slowed down. If she sped up, it sped up.

Not until they reached Omen Lane did the truck change its pattern. As Madison pressed her brake to navigate the turn, the truck kept at its current speed. Never slowing, it missed her bumper by mere inches.

"What is your problem!" she screamed in frustration, holding down long and hard on the horn.

Brash stood on the porch when they arrived at the house. An anxious expression creased the planes of his handsome face.

"I was starting to worry."

"So were we," Madison confided as he opened the car door for her.

With his help, they made short work of getting the groceries unloaded and into the house. While the other women sorted the items and put them way, Brash went back for the final bag. He motioned for his wife to join him.

"We had company," she said as they lingered at the Expedition. "A black two-ton truck. Windows so dark I couldn't see inside. It followed us all the way into town and all the way back."

"Any idea who was inside?"

"Some giant of a man with an attitude. He came stalking into the grocery store, looking all big and bad with his dark sunglasses, muddy snake guards, and a Carhartt jacket. Whoever he is, his reputation precedes him. The store fell into one of those uneasy silences, like they half-expected him to take out his gun and shoot up the place."

"What did he do?"

"He was headed my way, but Granny Bert and Miss Virgie created a diversion." At his horrified expression, Madison shook her head. "Don't ask. It bought us just enough time to get out to the truck and peal out of the parking lot, but it didn't take him long to catch up. He all but kissed my bumper as I turned down the lane. He kept going into the ranch entrance."

"You okay?"

"My nerves are tied in a knot, but other than that, we're all fine. He didn't make any direct overtures. But he definitely wanted me to know he was there."

Brash looked as thoughtful as he did concerned. He gave her shoulder an encouraging squeeze as his eyes left hers to scan the horizon.

"Someone's been watching us all day. I've only gotten a couple of glimpses of them. Mostly flashes of sunlight against metal."

Madison sucked in a quick breath. "A gun?"

Brash shrugged his shoulders. "Could be binoculars. I saw brief movement and a flash of red one time. Mostly, I can *feel* their eyes upon us."

"I know what you mean," she murmured, acknowledging the eerie sensation inching down her spine. "I feel them watching us now."

"Best I can tell, they use that ridge to spy on us. There's a hunting blind over to the far right. I think that's their cover."

"But isn't that on Dom's side of the property?" Madison asked. "I know it's still part of the ranch, but I thought his acreage was excluded from the hunting program."

"It is. But that doesn't keep someone from coming onto his side of the fence, especially when he's not here to defend his boundary."

"Wouldn't that be considered trespassing?"

"I'm not sure. I haven't read the will in its entirety or know how the deeds are worded. That's probably a question for a lawyer."

Remembering the overheard conversation in town, Madison asked, "When you were looking over the will, did you see a clause about the heirs not being able to contest it without forfeiting their inheritance?"

He nodded his dark head. "Yes. It's a very oddly worded will. It's like Phillip Perkins expected his heirs to fight over his legacy and tried to block them at every turn."

Madison considered his words. "So, if

someone can't contest the will for himself," she concluded, "he could try convincing another heir not to accept his portion of the inheritance. Either way, the first twelve heirs would be the sole owners. Thirteen and beyond would lose out."

Brash agreed with her analysis. "I have no idea why the man would put such a clause into his will, but it appears that is the case."

Like Brash, she discreetly scanned the horizon around them. "Strange family," Madison murmured.

"An understatement, I'm sure. My guess is that the 'someone' spying on us is a member of the Perkins family. At the very least, it's someone who works for them."

"But why?" Madison wondered aloud.

"My gut feeling is that something else is going on here. Something outside the realm of a big game ranch."

"You mean something outside the realm of the law." It wasn't a question.

He nodded curtly. "My guess is marijuana. In a ranch this size, it would be easy to hide a large crop. When Miss Virgie and I went up to the main house, I saw signs of an irrigation system. In land this arid, it could be for anything. Stock ponds. Food plots for the game animals. Grazing grass for the livestock. Or," he lifted one shoulder in speculation, "it could be for grass of a completely different nature. My bet is on the latter."

Lips pursed, Madison agreed. "It sounds like Uncle George wasn't a part of the covert operation, and the powers that be intend to exclude Dom, as well."

"That's my hypothesis. With Dom convinced the place is cursed and afraid to accept his share of the inheritance, ownership would fall back to the first twelve heirs. They could expand their operation and not have the worry of defection within their own ranks, so to speak."

"How do we prove it?"

"I'm going to start a surveillance of my own. I'll accept Terrance Perkins' offer of hunting the game ranch. I'll make it clear that I intend to do an evening hunt on this side of the game fence to compare the two."

"Smart. That way they'll know you're out there and won't be roaming the ridge at the same time."

"I can't promise that," he said, an enigmatic crook in his auburn brow. He went on to explain, "I plan on staying well after dark. Past legal hunting hours, but prime snooping hours."

"Not alone, you won't," Madison protested. "I'm coming with you!"

"But the other women..."

"Are competent and capable, and deadly with a firearm. Don't let their age fool you."

Brash was reluctant to agree. "I don't like the idea of leaving them here alone after dark. Especially for an extended period of time."

Madison was just as insistent. "I don't like the idea of you out there alone, facing who knows what."

Avoiding a direct argument, Brash hedged

with, "First, I have to set it up with Terrance. I'll tell him I plan to hunt tomorrow afternoon on Dom's side of the fence. That gives us a day to come up with a workable plan."

"As long as that plan includes us going together, I'm good with it."

Again, he chose to gloss over her comment. "Come on. Let's get this last bag into the house," Brash said.

"And then what?"

"I want to explore more of the area around the house again." Before she could ask, he intercepted her request. "And, yes. This time you can come with me."

She bestowed a bright smile upon her husband. "See? That didn't hurt at all."

Having taken the rear exit from the house, their exploration led them beyond the tool shed and the cluster of cottonwood trees serving as the backyard. Behind that, the land spread out like a warm chocolate chip cookie, mimicking the color and the stubbled texture but without the sweetness. The imposing house stood between them and the mountain ridge, offering Brash and Madison a respite from prying eyes as they ventured into the stubs.

"I never knew land could be so flat," Madison murmured, unimpressed with the way nothingness stretched in every direction, each section as flat and lifeless as the next.

"Don't let the optical illusion fool you. It may look flat, but there are deep canyons and arroyos cut through that expanse out there. Ridges and cliffs, just not as steep as the mountain in front of the house."

"You're kidding."

"They aren't as tall," he agreed, "but that doesn't mean they aren't out there. You can be walking along, thinking there's nothing but flat surface all around, and suddenly, the earth drops off into a deep ravine. Those ravines may be hiding ledges and caverns, even small streams, or, most likely at this time of year, dried up watering holes. Just looking out across the land, you can't see any trees, but that doesn't mean they aren't there. They may not be the tall pines and leafy varieties you're used to back home, but there are trees out there."

"But not on top of the mesas," she said, testing out Granny Bert's insistent claim.

"Very few. Trees seek water. Out here, most of the water is at the lower elevations of a canyon or ravine, not on top of a mesa. Most of the mountains are covered with rocks."

Madison didn't mention the movement she thought she had seen last night. Perhaps it had been her imagination. After the stress of a long drive, that rude awakening by a chilling cry, and the sleeplessness that followed, her mind could have been playing tricks on her. Exhaustion and overwrought nerves did strange things to the body. Even stranger things to the mind.

With enough denial, she might be able to convince herself of just that. Until then, she would remain silent.

"How far can we see from here?" she wondered aloud. She looked back at the house, now growing smaller in the distance. They had already come farther than she realized.

"Hard to say. Probably several miles." They continued to walk, until Brash asked, "Can you feel that? We're starting a slight decent, even though it looked completely flat from the house."

"You're right. We're going downhill." As her heels slid slightly on the descending rocks, she threw another glance backward. Only the top portion of the house was visible now.

"Watch your step," he cautioned. "It's getting rockier."

"Steeper, too," she said, sucking in her breath as she slid once again.

"Steady, now," Brash said, reaching out a helping hand.

Less than twenty feet ahead, the ground simply stopped. Madison found they stood on the slab of a rocky outcropping. A deep ravine cut through the earth below, lined with ragged limestone edges and hiding a small copse of trees.

"See what I mean?" Brash quirked an eyebrow as he gestured to the scene below.

"If you're trying not to sound condescending, you're failing miserably," she shot back. "You don't—"

"Shh." He flipped his hand over, signaling for her to be quiet.

She pretended outrage. "Don't tell me to be—"

Before she could protest further, Brash shook his finger in caution. Madison realized he was serious.

Stepping up close beside him, she stopped talking and strained to listen.

The faint sound of voices drifted up from the ravine. It took a moment to decipher that the fragmented words were spoken in Spanish. Brash took a tentative step closer, sending a small spray of pebbles over the edge of the outcrop where they stood.

The voices hushed.

Concern creased Madison's forehead as she reached out to clutch his arm. He looked back and shook his head, a silent assurance for her not to worry.

She did, regardless.

When no further sounds came from below, Brash signaled for her to retreat. Neither spoke until they were well into the incline, headed back toward the house.

"Brash," she said in a loud whisper, "what is going on? Who was that down there?"

His answer was terse. "I don't know." He gave her a hand as she maneuvered the tricky terrain, her shoes again sliding on the rocky surface. Back on flat land, he frowned. "If you're going with me tomorrow night," he glanced down at her feet, "you need shoes with treads."

"So, you'll take me?"

Brash glanced backward. Already swallowed up by the illusion of flatness, the decline and the ravine beyond weren't visible from here.

"Yeah," he agreed thoughtfully. "I'll take you with me. It may take both of us to figure out what's going on around here."

"Who do you think that was back there?" Madison asked.

"I have no clue. It could have been someone who works here at the ranch."

"Do you think they were trying to sneak up on us from the rear?"

"I doubt it. I didn't see an easy means of climbing up from the ravine. The walls were too steep. I'm sure there's an easier path somewhere, but not there."

"Then why were people down there?"

"Again, no clue. Maybe they were checking on livestock."

"Could you understand any of their words?"

"No. Could you?"

Madison shook her head. "Even if they hadn't been so faint, I know very little Spanish. I just knew they were voices."

"That's about all I could hear, too," he agreed.

"This is getting stranger and stranger."

"I agree. Until we have something more to work with, there's no way to put any of this together that makes any sense."

"Maybe if we can get a good night's rest, things will be clearer in the morning."

"We can hope." He didn't sound convinced.

10

Megan spent most of the day admiring her tiny companion. Baby Faith's milky skin and petite blond curls fascinated the teenager. She was in love with the silly faces the baby made and giggled every time Faith cooed or attempted a smile.

At eighteen, Brash's only biological child was already a stunning beauty, with thick, long tresses of dark-auburn hair. Megan credited her vibrant personality and effervescent sass to the red undertones in her hair. Brash credited his ex-wife for their daughter's beauty and charm, even though her coloring came from the deCordova side of the family.

Brash and Shannon had married young (it was considered the only right thing to do back then) and tried making a go of it. They gave up within three years. To their surprise, without the petty arguments and trivial static that had driven them apart, they became close friends. The divorced couple made a pact to raise their only child together, even if from two households. When Shannon later married his best friend from childhood, Brash couldn't have been happier. Matt Aikman was the only man he trusted to care for his daughter and to help mold her character.

Long before Brash could woo Madison and convince her he was no longer the playboy she crushed on in high school, Megan and Bethani became fast friends. Megan was a regular at the Reynolds' dinner table before Brash was invited for a first meal. Having their children get along so well made blending their family so much easier. With Blake completing their circle, the Reynolds-deCordovas made for the perfect family.

Taking her babysitting responsibilities to heart, Megan spent the better part of the day holding the baby or simply watching her sleep. She kept her ear pods on low and didn't get absorbed in her phone, devoting her full attention to her tiny charge.

Genny and Hope returned home with a good report from the doctor. The baby had nothing more than a stuffy nose and a touch of the common cold. Seeing the worry lines on Genny's face and the puffy skin around her eyes, Megan offered to stay while Genny took a short nap. One look at her "aunt" told Megan she needed the rest.

Cutter came in not long after, and Megan saw the exhaustion on his face, as well. With both girls still sleeping, she offered to cook an early dinner for the couple.

"You don't have to, Meg. I'll let Genny sleep a while longer, and I'll rustle us up something to eat."

"I like cooking. I know I can't do nearly anything as fancy as Genny, her being a professional and all, but I can hold my own in the kitchen," the girl boasted. "Pasta and chicken sound okay?"

"After the day I've had, macaroni and cheese from a box sounds okay."

"Was there a fire?" she asked the chief of the volunteer fire department.

"No, but there was a wreck on the highway, and we had to do traffic control." He ticked off some of the day's events. "There's some new business coming into town, and the owner asked me to check out the building to see if it was up to code or posed any fire dangers. The ambulance called for a lift-assist when Twila Jones fell out of her wheelchair."

"That's Latisha grandmother, right?" Megan broke in. She and Latisha were friends. "Is she okay?"

"Nothing serious. She was reaching for a cannister of cookies on a high shelf and tried to stand. The medics on the ambulance weren't stout enough to lift her on her own, so they called for us. She insisted I stay for coffee and some of the cookies. Since they were homemade, I took her up on the offer." Cutter flashed the smile that still made him a heartthrob to women young and old, despite his status as a happily married family man.

"I don't blame you. She's a good cook!" Megan began slicing the raw chicken breasts into strips. "What new business? Where's it going to be?"

"The old dry cleaners' building in Juliet."

"The one on the corner?"

"That's the one. The representative that met me there today was hush-hush on what kind of business is going in, but he carried on about all the parking and how the owners had big plans for it. I didn't see any major concerns, so they plan to start renovations immediately."

"I hope it's something good, and not another feed or supply store." Behind her sparkling gold and silver glasses, Megan rolled her eyes.

"Gotta give the customers what they want." Cutter grinned. "This is farm and ranching country. Not much use for some high-dollar department store here."

"Why not? You know everyone just drives into Bryan-College Station to do their shopping. If there were more stores here, we wouldn't have to spend our money somewhere else."

"You have a point, but I'm no merchant. I weld, work a ranch, and fight fires."

"Don't forget you pitch in at your wife's restaurant and help take care of two precious daughters."

His smile turned rueful. "Maybe that's why I'm so tired. Hope hasn't slept well the past two nights."

"Go rest. I've got this. And I have the baby monitor on if one of the girls wakes up."

"You sure?"

"Of course."

Her offer was too good to refuse. "I'll just crash in the chair over there."

While Megan browned the chicken and boiled water for penne pasta, Cutter sprawled out in a large leather chair and dozed. Before long, she heard Genny come down, and the two moved to the couch, where they snuggled and spoke in low voices.

Chopping vegetables for a salad and stirring up a cream sauce to pull the pasta dish together, Megan listened to the baby monitor more than she did the couple's conversation. She wove a few daydreams about when she would one day have a baby and loving husband of her own. It would be after college, of course. Maybe after she started her law practice, if that was what she settled on for her career. She was torn between being a lawyer or being a lab technician. Both sounded interesting.

A few snippets of the conversation on the couch drifted her way, but Megan chose not to listen. One word, however, caught her ear.

"I'm afraid they might sue," Genny said worriedly to her husband.

As a potential lawyer-in-the-making, mention of a lawsuit snagged Megan's attention.

"Hey, now," Cutter said, shifting to look down at the woman crooked in his arm. "Don't be borrowing troubles. You have no reason to believe they'll take their complaints that far."

"I've had irate customers before. This was something entirely different."

"You weren't even there. You weren't to blame for the man's clumsiness," Cutter reminded her.

"He claims otherwise. He says the floor was slick and had no sign to warn him not to walk there. My restaurant, my employees, so my fault." She passed her hand between the two of them. "*Our* fault."

"Wasn't Thelma on her way to get a mop to

clean it all up, after the kid spilled his drink?"

"That's what I understand. But the man said there should have been a sign, or at least a chair or something to make people go around the mess."

"He couldn't see it?" Cutter looked skeptical.

Genny sighed. "I guess not. Dierra said he rushed through lunch and was very demanding the entire time. He kept calling for a server to bring this, take that back, refill this, do that. When she brought him the bill, he jumped up and started for the register, not paying any attention to the drink all over the floor in front of him."

"What did you say his name was?"

"Lawrence Norris, like the famous guy up the road. No relations to the karate expert turned actor, I'm sure. This Norris seems the kind who would play that connection to the hilt," she smirked.

Cutter frowned. "We paid his ER bill. The doctor said there was nothing wrong with him."

"He claims there was a delayed complication. He threw his hip out and is now seeing a chiropractor. And then there's the matter of public humiliation, mental distress, and his dry-cleaning bill."

Cutter snorted. "Sounds to me like he has one of those personal injury lawyers. The kind that only get paid if you get paid, so they go after everything and anything."

As Megan turned away to stir the sauce, she considered what a career as an attorney might be like. While everyone deserved justice, for every case won, there had to be a loser.

Perhaps, she decided, she should rethink her options. She could always specialize in a specific field of law. Fight for good causes, like her dad did. Child advocacy came to mind. She loved children and believed they should be cherished and protected, and never used as leverage or as means to an end.

She pondered what a career in child advocacy might be like until her phone binged with a message from Bethani.

OMG! You will not BELIEVE what just happened!

Megan tapped out a quick reply.

What?

Bubbles appeared before the text arrived.

Cruella Lewis just accused me of food poisoning! Said I did something to her order, and she's filing a lawsuit. How am I supposed to tell Aunt Genny??

Megan spared a glance toward the living room. Genny was already stressed. How *would* she react to the news?

The telephone rang as Megan was tapping out her reply. When she saw the look on Genny's face, she amended her words.

Maybe you won't have to. Phone just rang, and I think she knows.

Bethani replied with a string of emojis, ranging from tears, shaking her head, and prayers.

A few moments later, the news was confirmed. Genny hung up the phone and turned a stricken face to her husband.

"That was Trenessa. That toad Myrna Lewis

claims she got food poisoning today at *New Beginnings*. She stooped so low as to blame Bethani for it! All Beth does is deliver the food, not prepare it! And I highly doubt the kitchen was responsible, either. Myrna is just an old sourpuss, and no doubt her stomach has had enough of her inner poison!"

"Myrna Lewis claims she's sick? I saw her this afternoon. She looked perfectly fine!" After making the statement, Cutter clarified his words. "Well, as fine as possible for her. But she definitely wasn't sick."

Fully agitated, Genny jumped to her feet. "She's always been out to get me. Madison and I both. This way, she can hurt both of us with one fell swoop."

"She can try, but it doesn't mean she'll succeed. She can lodge a complaint with the health department, but they won't just take her word for it. They'll do an investigation and see if anyone else had the same symptoms." He stood and took his wife into his arms. "Don't get worked up over this, darlin'. We'll call Shawn Bryant first thing in the morning and let him take care of it. He's been your lawyer since you opened, and you've never had to use him, yet."

"First, it's Lawrence Norris, and now this! What is this? Pick on Genny Montgomery Month?" the blonde wailed.

"I didn't mean to eavesdrop," Megan said tentatively, stepping into the adjacent room. "Bethani texted and told me what was going on. Everyone knows how Myrna Lewis is. Her life is miserable, so she makes it her goal to share her misery."

"But she's married to the sweetest man! Why should she be miserable?" Genny protested.

"Her looks? Her late sister? Her personality?" the teen guessed. "Who knows why she is the way she is? But she's wrong, of course. She may have an upset stomach, but it's not from something she ate at *New Beginnings*. She's nothing but a fat, old toad. She probably ate a tainted fly with her forked tongue."

Genny attempted a weak smile. "Thanks, Meg, but we all know how loud and demanding she can be. She may be proved wrong, but she can ruin my business in the meantime!"

"I doubt that," the girl all but snorted. "You have loyal customers. Everyone loves you, Aunt Genny, which is probably why she hates you so much. Her own business didn't do so well, and no one likes her, even Derron. If her own nephew can see through her, you know everyone else does, too."

"But to pull Bethani into this! How low can you go?"

"She is awfully round and low to the ground," Megan pointed out, a mischievous twinkle in her eye. "I'd say she can go pretty low."

A round of laughter did them all good, and Megan encouraged the couple to eat while the girls were still napping. After hugging her 'aunt' goodbye and offering heartfelt assurances, she let herself out the door.

Now to console her stepsister and best friend...

11

Back at 1313 Omen Lane, dinner was a casserole from the freezer and what was left of Miss Wanda's cake. After a few games of Chicken Foot, the group called it a night and retired to their prospective rooms.

By morning, their sleep uninterrupted by piercing screams, everyone felt more refreshed.

"I spotted some blackberries in the freezer," Miss Sybil said. "I think Wanda and I may make a cobbler today."

Brash smiled as he patted his trim waistline. "If I didn't know better, I'd say you ladies are trying to fatten me up on this trip."

"You can stand to gain a pound or two," Wanda granted him. "But mostly, we just need something to do. Cooking is the best cure for boredom."

He gave her his most charming smile. "Far be it from me to argue with that logic."

"Which is why I do my best to never be bored," Madison joked. Although she was a good cook in her own right, she preferred to take a back seat to experts like Genny and Granny Bert. She had always heard that too many cooks could spoil the stew, so she was more than willing to stand back and allow them to shine.

"You stay busy enough, stirring up trouble and finding dead bodies," Miss Virgie pointed out.

"Hey!" Maddy protested playfully. "Might I remind you that this current trouble was of your making, not mine."

The older woman disagreed. "I didn't make the trouble. Dom did."

"You just delivered it to my doorstep."

"Along with a tidy sum of money," Miss Virgie added. "Don't forget the money."

"Believe me, I haven't."

"That money," Brash agreed, "is the only reason I agreed to this cockamamie scheme in the first place. I've gotta tell you, Miss Virgie. Nothing about this case makes any sense."

"You'll get no argument from me. Then, again, Dom always was a strange one."

"I've never asked," Madison said, approaching the delicate topic tentatively, "but do you mind telling me about your first husband? Until just a few months ago, I never knew you had been married before Mr. Hank."

"It wasn't a long marriage," Virgie explained. "I met Robert Perkins just before he went off to the Army. Hank and I had been sweet on each other most of our lives but at the time, we were on the outs."

"That's right," Granny Bert broke in on a

croon. "He was seeing Dorian Nettles at the time."

Virgie sent her friend a scathing look, but she ignored the interruption. "Robert came along, and he looked so dashing in his uniform, I suppose he just swept me off my feet. Call it a sense of misguided patriotism or romantic foolishness, but when he asked me to marry him before he set sail, I agreed. We came to the ranch for our honeymoon. Three months later, they told me there was some sort of mishap during training, and Robert had been killed."

"That's so sad!"

"It was. But the truth is, I never loved Robert. My heart belonged to Hank. We were married six months later and have been ever since."

"That's amazing that you kept up with Robert's cousin, only being married for such a short time," Brash commented.

"My younger cousin Loretta and I met the two of them at a dance. Loretta and Dom dated for a while so, truth be told, I got to know him better than I ever knew my own husband. When Loretta up and married someone else, Dom needed a shoulder to cry on. Hank didn't like it much, but I helped Dom through a dark time. After that, we kept in touch."

Madison smiled. "That was nice of you."

"Well, he was family of a sort. I didn't dare say as much to Hank, but that's how I saw it."

"Still, that was very commendable of you," Madison insisted.

Granny Bert grinned. "Don't let her fool you. It was her way of getting even with Hank for still being friends with Dorian."

"It's a small town. He couldn't very well be her enemy!" Virgie protested. "Especially since she married one of his friends. We were in the same social circle."

"You're a better woman than I am," Wanda said. "When my good-for-nothing husband started cheating on me with Pearl, I didn't care that we attended the same church or that we were both in the same Eastern Star Chapter. I blackballed her slimy ass—pardon my French—and ran her plumb out of town."

"And you did the right thing," Miss Sybil assured her. "No one liked her, anyways."

"No one but William." Quite candidly, Wanda admitted, "But then, he always did like anything in a skirt, and she liked to wear hers tight and short."

"Never mind that she was so pigeon-toed her knees knocked together when she walked, and her legs were the size of toothpicks," Granny Bert snickered.

"Like toothpicks stuck in an apple," Virgie agreed. "It's not like she had the figure to pull off that style."

"One thing about William," Wanda said with a grudging admittance, "he wasn't critical when it came to a woman's figure. He always said he judged a woman by—" She stopped abruptly, sliding a glance in Brash's direction. "I reckon it's too early in the morning for sexy talk. Maybe we should change the subject."

"Maybe so!" Brash agreed enthusiastically. He obliged without missing a beat. "I think Maddy and I will go over to the main ranch house again and take Terrance up on that offer of a hunt. This evening, we plan to sit in that blind on top of the ridge out front. We might be out well after dark. Anyone feel uncomfortable with those arrangements?"

"Not me," Miss Wanda said, reaching for another biscuit.

"Why would we object?" Virgie asked.

Brash couldn't help but feel it was a trick question. He proceeded with caution. "It would just be the four of you, here alone at the house."

"Just?" Granny Bert challenged, a glint coming into her eyes. "As in, just four defenseless, old women, against who knows what?"

Virgie took up the challenge, as well. "Or as, just four little old ladies against a sea of big, bad wolves?"

"Just us," Wanda pitched in, "without the benefit of a man to protect us?"

"Or just us, with what amounts to only one brain among the four of us?" Granny Bert added.

With a sardonic smile twisting his mouth, Brash said, "Actually, I meant just you ladies, without someone here to defend the outside world from your own particular brand of wrath."

Miss Sybil beamed her pleasure upon hearing his explanation. "Now, aren't you sweet."

"You're assuming someone might be foolish enough to cross us," Granny Bert snapped.

"True. Sad as it may be, the world is full of fools." Brash gave a long-suffering sigh.

"It's also sad that some of us at this table are

full of horse manure!" Granny Bert huffed. Wrinkles swam across her face as she broke into a sudden smile and elbowed him affectionately. "Nice save, by the way."

He started to protest, but quickly caved with a grin of his own. "A guy's gotta think on his feet with you ladies around. Sometimes, I think I'm out of my league among the four of you."

Virgie gave him a condescending look. "Only sometimes?"

"Okay, most of the time," he relented, laughing. The lawman pushed back from the table. "Ladies, that was a fine meal. Thank you. If you don't mind, I'll excuse myself."

"Not at all, and you are most welcome. Maddy, we'll do the dishes," Wanda insisted. "You go on with your man and take care of business. We've got this."

"Are you sure? I don't mind doing my share of kitchen duties."

"You've got more important matters to worry with. This is our contribution to the trip," Miss Sybil confirmed.

"If you're sure..."

"We are. Shoo!"

Terrance Perkins was nothing like Madison imagined. She was thinking along the same lines as the brute in the snake gaiters. Tall and thick, with a domineering personality to match his brusque voice. She imagined lots of flannel and a burly beard.

In reality, Terrance was a small man. The top

of his balding head barely reached Brash's broad shoulder. He had a pencil-thin mustache above a severe overbite. When he spoke, Madison detected the slight whistle that often accompanied a lisp.

"A true pleasure to meet you," he said, pumping her hand with more enthusiasm than warranted. She was hardly the First Lady of Texas, for goodness sake.

Keeping her thoughts to herself, Madison tolerated the invigorated handshake. "It's nice to meet you, too, Mr. Perkins."

"Please, call me Terrance. Would you care for some wine or a brandy? What about you, Brash? Care to join me in a drink?"

Terrance waved a slender hand to the elaborate bar behind them. He had ushered them into a very masculine-styled den, complete with a massive rock fireplace, leather-bound bar with matching furniture, and plenty of stuffed and mounted wildlife.

"It's a bit early in the day for me, but thanks," Brash said, waving away the offer. "Especially on a day I plan to go hunting. I don't believe in mixing bullets and booze."

"Ah, a truly wise man!" Terrance chortled, lifting his own highball glass in salute. "I hope that means you've decided to take me up on my offer? Decided to cut your losses on that side of the fence and hunt for a real trophy?" he asked with confidence. "Let me make a call and get that set up for you."

Madison didn't like the gleam of victory that

crept into his eyes.

In fact, she didn't like much about Terrance Perkins. The man gave off definite sleazeball vibes.

"Yes, and no," Brash answered. "I think I will take you up on your generous offer, but not today. I plan to hunt Dom's acreage this evening. I think I saw a nice set of horns moving along that mountain that faces the house." He pretended not to notice the decided look of displeasure replacing the victorious gleam. "I'm sure they're nothing compared to your breeding stock, but I thought it might be worth the effort."

"I doubt it," he said, the whistle even more evident as a snort. "George never bothered to improve his stock. He was content to take the culls we turned loose."

Madison wasn't too proud to play dumb. Genny normally played the part when they worked together, but her friend made it look simple enough. Surely, it couldn't be too hard. Madison went so far as to fluff her hair, stuff a stick of gum into her mouth, and give it a definite smack. "I'm just fascinated with the dynamics of a family ranch like yours," she gushed. "So, help me sort this all out. George, rest his poor soul, was your uncle. Right?"

"Correct."

"And he was Dom's uncle, too?"

"That's correct. Technically, George was my great uncle. He was the youngest of Phillip Perkins' seven sons, while my grandfather was the oldest. Dom and I are second cousins."

Madison crossed a long leg over her knee and

bounced it up and down. She seemed deep in thought. "But Dom's name is Hebert, not Perkins."

"His mother was Phillip's daughter," their host explained.

"Oh, so that explains it. I wondered how you were family but had different last names." She smiled brightly. "I think it's so nice that you're one big, happy family, all living here on the ranch together." The smile faltered. "Well, except for Dom. He lives in Louisiana. Or was it Texarkana? One of those Anas, anyway! I'm not very good with geography," she admitted with a wave of her hand. "But I guess that's only a temporary situation, right? He'll be moving here in no time, just as soon as he can get his affairs in order." Madison smacked her gum again for good measure. "He must have a really understanding wife."

She heard Brash smother a strangling sound and dared not look in his direction. She bounced her leg a few more times before making an abrupt request. "Do you have a little girl's room I can borrow?"

"Of course. Down the far hallway to your left. It's the first door on your right."

"You two go on with your macho talk. Don't let me stop you." She made a fluttering motion with her hands, holding her fingers over her head to indicate antlers.

Madison hurried from the heavily paneled den with no intentions of looking for the powder room. The first door she opened revealed a board room dominated by a long table with leather chairs all around. Huge screens and projectors lined the walls, indicating it also served as some sort of viewing room.

The second door led to an office. Making certain the hallway was clear, Madison slipped inside its confines. She rushed over to the desk and skimmed the papers atop it. Scattered in front of a computer screen were files and a cluttered stack of papers. Without knowing what she was looking for, she had no idea of what might be important. She took pictures with her cell phone, including a shot of the calendar pad. She couldn't help but notice that several dates were circled, while others were underlined. Some squares held notations and appointment reminders.

A quick search through the desk drawers revealed the usual mix of office necessities, along with one huge surprise. The locking mechanism on the bottom drawer was turned into the correct position, but a file was caught in the rail, preventing the lock from engaging. Madison darted a guilty glance toward the door before sliding the drawer open.

She sucked in an audible gasp as the bulky file folder drooped open. A thick stack of money was bound by a rubber band and carelessly stuffed inside, atop two more identical stacks of money.

For whatever reason, Madison was reluctant to touch the bills, but she saw a healthy mix of hundreds in with the tens and twenties. She snapped more photos before sliding the drawer shut and moving on.

The upright file cabinet in the corner was securely locked and left no options for snooping. No clues awaited her within the locked gun display or on the near-barren bookshelves, which held more photos than actual books. Deciding not to press her luck, Madison slipped stealthily into the hallway.

She thought she was home free until a deep voice boomed from behind, "Who are you, and what are you doing in Mr. Perkins' office?"

Madison said a silent prayer as she mentally prepared herself to play the part of an airhead again. Don't be the brute, don't be the brute. Please don't be the brute. She was already smacking on her gum when she turned around with a falsely bright smile, her hand over her chest.

"Oh, thank goodness someone came along!" And double thanks that you're not the brute! Though tall and brooding, this man didn't look nearly as formidable as the man from yesterday. "I'm afraid I'm lost." She simpered just a little, hoping to sound believable. "I went to the little girl's rooms to tinkle, and now I can't find my way back to the room with all the stuffed animals. Not the soft, fluffy kind, mind you, like the ones on our bed back home. The kind with big horns and glass eyes. Just being in the room gives me the heebie-jeebies." She shivered for good measure.

"You aren't supposed to be in Mr. Perkins' office," he said, clearly unimpressed with her plight.

"I didn't mean to be in there, either! I'm trying to get back to my husband and Mr. Perkins, but there are too many doors in this place. They all look the same." Madison deliberately turned in the opposite direction of the den. "Do I go left or right up here? I'm as lost as a blind goose in a hailstorm!"

"It's behind you," the man said, his expression still flat. He placed his hands on her shoulders and forcibly turned her in the correct direction. He did not, however, release her once she was repositioned.

Madison attempted to dislodge his hold by dipping her shoulder, but his grip was secure. She considered calling out for Brash, but the sound of her husband's voice made it unnecessary.

"There you are, Buttercup." His voice sounded almost like a caress, but there was no warmth in the blazing sizzle of his eyes. The icy-cold heat of his glare was solely directed at the man who dared manhandle his wife. That man was about the same height as Brash and heavier, but that mattered none to the lawman.

Brash moved like a cheetah, his actions swift and deliberate, and very much in the man's face. He deftly pried the other man's fingers away, crushing them in his palm until the man winced. Brash gave him a withering glare before dismissing him like a pesky child.

"Turned around again, Buttercup?" he asked. He pulled Madison away, placing his solid body between her and her manhandler.

"You know me and directions." She tried for an upbeat chirp, but it was sadly lacking. She darted a glance over her shoulder. The man followed close on their heels.

Seemingly unconcerned, Brash didn't bother

acknowledging him.

Terrance Perkins waited for them in the doorway of the den, drink still in hand. The thin smile on his lips never quite reached his eyes.

"Ah, there you are," he said to Madison. He glanced down at his watch, a none-too-subtle hint that she had taken too long in the powder room. When displeased, as he clearly was now, his lisp was more noticeable. "Malcolm," he said to the man behind them. "Our guests were about to leave. Would you mind showing them out?"

Like a trained puppy, the big man jumped to do his bidding. "Yes, sir, Mr. Perkins."

Brash would not be hurried. He took his time thanking their host and pretending enthusiasm over his hunt there the next day.

"Anything for a sports legend such as yourself." The gushing words seemed sincere.

Madison made some inane comment about his lovely but huge house having too many doors that looked the same. After an over-exuberant goodbye, she turned to face Malcolm, popping her gum as she did so. She bit back a smile when she saw the flash of irritation cross his face, but he said not a word as he led the couple to the door.

She noted that he still favored his injured hand.

The moment they were in the truck and heading away from the house, Madison turned to her husband and said, "Oh, my gosh, Brash! You will not believe what I found in Terrance Perkins' desk!"

"You snooped in the man's desk? No wonder

Malcolm had a death grip on your shoulder!"

"He had no right touching me, b—"

"I agree," her husband interrupted, his expression dark. "I should have broken his entire hand, not just a finger."

Her eyes widened. "You broke his finger?"

His shrug looked uncomfortable. "Possibly."

Madison was temporarily distracted by the realization of her husband's sheer power. He had shown her nothing but tenderness and love, but she had always known that he could be a formidable opponent when pushed.

Shaking away the sense of awe she felt over his carefully controlled strength, she waved her hand to steer herself back on track. "That's not the point right now. The point is, I found thousands of dollars, all bundled up with a rubber band, in Perkins' desk drawer!"

His calm reply wasn't the reaction she had envisioned. "And?"

"And what?" She was miffed that he didn't recognize the magnitude of her discovery.

"That's what I'm asking. There's no law against keeping cash in your desk."

"There is if it's illegally gained cash, and I bet you my bottom dollar, that's exactly what it was!"

"Was it clearly counterfeit?"

She frowned at the question. "No, of course not."

"Was there any sort of notation, indicating it was illegally obtained?"

"You mean like a neon post-it note written in

blood?" Her tone dripped sarcasm. "No. But keeping that much cash on hand is suspicious, in and of itself!"

"The Perkins' Ranch is a high-dollar game ranch, sweetheart. Their hunts pull in thousands of dollars for a single animal. How do you know that wasn't money from a legitimate guest, waiting to be deposited in the bank?"

"For one thing, there was no bank deposit slip. No bank bag. And I rather doubt that anyone who can afford that kind of money for a hunting trip would literally pay in tens and twenties. I even saw some fives in there."

"Again, that proves nothing. For all we know, he heads up a charitable donation for needy kids at Christmas. Maybe they had a county fair, and he sold chances for a side of beef. The thing is, now your fingerprints are on that money and are proof that you were snooping. If any of that money comes up missing, he could blame you."

"Pul-leeze," she said in an exasperated voice. "I'm married to a law officer. I watch crime shows on TV and work part-time for a private investigator. In lieu of gloves, I know to use my clothes to keep from leaving prints. This isn't my first time to snoop, you know."

"No, I don't know," he replied. His voice was stern as he added, "And I don't want to, seeing as I'm bound by law to report criminal activity."

Madison wore a stubborn expression on her face. "Terrance Perkins' activity may not be obviously criminal, but you do have to admit, it does look suspicious. Some of those bills looked grungy and wrinkled, like they had spent the last ten years stuffed in a mattress or something. Some were old issue. That much money—three bundles of it, mind you! — stuffed randomly into a file folder just looks suspicious."

Brash's eyes narrowed in speculation. "I'll give you that," he relented. "It does look suspicious."

12

"Where did these come from?" Madison asked that afternoon, peering down at the contraptions Brash buckled around her calves.

"I found them in a closet," he admitted. "But no worries. I don't think George will object if we borrow them."

"Don't think that charming smile of yours will distract me from what these really are," his wife warned. "These are snake gaiters!"

"They are. Would you prefer not wearing them?"

Aggravated by his reasonable demeanor, Madison refused a direct answer. "Just hurry it up," she grumbled.

Brash chuckled. "That's what I thought you said."

"You have extra flashlights, right? The satellite phone? A general knowledge of where we're going and how we're getting there?"

"Slow down. I think you're getting a little worked up here."

"Worked up? That big brute followed me to and from town and crowded my bumper as a warning. Malcolm, or whatever his name is, caught me snooping and tried forcing me back to the den. Terrance was clearly unhappy with your announcement that we were hunting Dom's place this evening, and it had nothing to do with hero worship." She named off her concerns one by one. "The entire time we've been here, someone has been watching us, and we both know it's not simply a nosy neighbor like we have back home! Now we're about to sit out in an open field and walk back in the dark. Where there are rattlesnakes, coyotes, and who knows what else. And as if all that isn't enough, one of those elses is whatever—or whoever— let out that blood-chilling scream night before last. So, yeah, I guess I am getting a little worked up."

"You don't have to go with me."

"Of course, I do! I don't want you going out there alone."

"I'm a big boy, sweetheart. I can take care of myself." Leg guards secure, he rose to his full six-foot-one-inch stature and gently placed his hands upon her shoulders. "I appreciate that you want to go along and make sure I'm safe, but you don't have to. You can stay here and keep an eye on the others."

"We've already discussed this. I'm coming with you."

"Fine. Then I'll ask you the same questions. Flashlight? Emergency kit? Extra water and protein bars?"

"Aye, aye, Cap'n," she replied smartly.

"And for the record, we won't exactly be out in an open field. We'll be in a deer blind."

"On top of a high, flat plateau, so it's sort of the same thing."

Shaking his head at her stubbornness, he pointed out, "You didn't name off the most important thing of all. At least we'll both be armed."

Madison wasn't comforted by the thought. She lifted one shoulder with a weary sigh. "There is that."

The two set out in Brash's pickup truck, following the rough sketch Dom provided. They drove as far as the road allowed, which was only about a fourth way up the mountain. The rest was done by foot.

Her boots slid several times on the steep terrain. Brash encouraged her to find rocks and exposed roots to aid in her climb, but mostly, she used his arm. The formation almost seemed to be stacked in layers, offering bands of flat ground winding upward. In many places, harsh elements and wildlife had carved trails of a sort, making it easier to traverse.

Still, by the time they crested the top, she was out of breath, sweating, and short tempered. It aggravated her that Brash made scaling the rugged incline look so simple. She struggled with every step.

Already, she was dreading going back down. By then, it would be dark. Everyone knew that snakes preferred the dark of night to the light of day.

"Let's catch our breaths before climbing up into the deer stand."

"More climbing?" Even she could hear the whine in her voice.

"A ladder makes it easier."

Still, she grumbled, "Says the lawman who keeps in shape."

"Gotta stay in shape to run down all those criminals."

"I would make some glib comment about all the hardened criminals in The Sisters stealing cookies, but I'm too tired."

"That, and because you know all too well that there is a criminal element there, no matter what we'd all like to believe."

"Again, too tired to comment."

When she gave the nod that she was ready, Brash led the way over the mountain's rocky crest. There were a few nubby shrubs and bushes scattered across the cap-rock and one huge, lonesome rectangular box sitting atop a cluster of metal legs.

"*That's* a deer stand?" she asked, forgetting for a moment to keep her voice low. "It's like a tiny house!"

"Deer stands have come a long way," Brash grinned. "This isn't the top-of-line version, but it's probably what they offer on the game ranch. I'll go up first to check things out."

"What kind of things?"

"Spiders," he answered as he started up the ladder. She couldn't be certain, but she imagined it was something larger than a spider he scouted.

In no time, his long legs delivered him to the

door of the tiny house in the sky. He left his rifle and backpack inside before coming down to assist his wife.

"Wow!" Madison said as she stepped inside. Unlike most stands she had crawled into with Brash, the platform outside made it easy to walk upright through the door. "This is humongous! And very nice."

It was nothing like she expected. Two padded rolling chairs offered easy access to every window. All were covered with plexiglass. Indoor-outdoor carpet on the floor kept the chill at bay and helped muffle noises. A large plastic storage box could be used as a seat, a table, or even a child-sized bed. There were even portable butane heaters to provide warmth on the coldest of days.

It struck her odd that there was a blanket neatly folded atop the box, and what might have been a one-burner camp stove peeking from behind. Did someone really cook while on the deer stand? Wouldn't the deer shy away from the smell?

And coffee? Really? She saw a stove-top percolator style pot on the floor, a cup draped upside down upon it.

"This is executive style hunting for the big shots who can't rough it like the rest of us," Brash told her.

"Very nice," she repeated, "if not a bit messy. Someone didn't clean up after themselves."

Brash took in the array of food wrappers, empty water bottles, and a pile of clothes in one corner. He also noted that some of the wrappers looked full. "It does look like someone has been up here recently."

"So much for respecting the boundaries of Dom's property," she grumbled.

"I don't see any spent shell casing. And with all those wrappers, I don't think whoever was up here was concerned about being quiet. My guess is they weren't deer hunting."

"Spying, you think?"

Brash eyed the evidence again. "That, or possibly living up here."

"In a deer stand?"

"It beats living in the woods."

"I suppose," Madison murmured, looking around with fresh eyes. That would explain the blanket and the coffee pot. With carpet, windowpanes, and butane heaters, a boxed-in stand beat sleeping in the elements. Some of the water bottles, she noted, were unopened. "I hope that's not the case," she said sympathetically. "That would be sad."

"Definitely not the best solution, but desperation calls for desperate measures."

Once they were settled, they did little talking. Brash had no real intention of hunting, but they both enjoyed watching the wildlife. From high on their perch, they had a good view of the ranch in general, and of George's house in particular.

"I have to admit," Madison whispered, leaning into her husband's arm. "The view is amazing from up here. I can literally see for miles. From up here, I can see that the land is far from flat. There are canyons and ravines you can't see from ground level."

"See that winding river over there? That's the Pecos," he pointed out. "It dumps into the Rio Grande at the Amistad Reservoir, just west of the Seminole Canyon State Park. That's probably the reservoir we see from here."

"Gorgeous," she said with awe. "It really is a beautiful area, even with all the rocks and thorns."

"It is."

She enjoyed the scenery for a long moment, marveling at the subtle shades that painted the landscape. The sheer vastness of the area left her speechless. It reminded her of a piece of Western artwork.

Later, after swinging her gaze toward the gray stone house on Omen Lane, she said, "I hate to say it, but this also makes an ideal place to spy on us from. Look at how well you can see the house from here."

"I thought the same thing."

Madison also discovered she had good cell reception from the deer stand, so she spent much of the next two hours texting. It came as no surprise that Myrna Lewis was stirring up trouble again, but this time, she had Bethani and Genny in her crosshairs. Madison exchanged texts with both of them, offering her support and asking if she needed to come home. Both told her she'd better not dare. Blake assured his mom that he had his sister's back, but their conversation thread soon drifted to his own life. With Blake's high school football career now over, he was looking forward to his true love of baseball. Several colleges had tried luring him into their athletic program, but he had yet to commit. There was also his interest in acting to consider, which Granny Bert took full credit for. He wanted a university that could offer him both.

Madison also texted Derron to make sure he had things under control at *In a Pinch,* while Brash checked in with the police station. Most of his attention, however, was directed to the view. He pretended to be admiring the wildlife and the miles of rough country stretched out before them, but Madison knew better. He was on alert, watching for any signs of danger.

As darkness crowded in around them, she snuggled closer to Brash's side. Daylight leaked from the sky and smudged in the corners, making things distorted and ill shaped. Moments before, Madison could detect the spindly branches of a small yaupon bush behind the stand. Now, it looked like a dark, squat monster with the arms of an octopus.

"How long do we need to wait?" she whispered.

"I want it fully dark before we get down."

"You do realize I'm going to break my neck going down this mountain. At the very least, my ankle."

"You'll do no such thing," he whispered back. "Have faith."

"But I won't be able to see a thing!"

"The moon is fairly bright. Plus, I have night-vision goggles for you. My backup pair isn't very good, but it's better than nothing. Here. Have a protein bar while we wait."

They sat in the virtual silence, hearing only the movement of wind through the spikes of brush and rock. Out of nowhere, the sound of voices drifted on the air. Like the day before, the words themselves were indecipherable, but both could tell they were spoken in Spanish.

"Who is that?" she mouthed almost silently.

She felt his broad shoulders lift in a shrug. "Workers?"

"On Dom's property?"

Brash chanced a quiet whisper. "The wind may be blowing the words from further away."

She raised a dubious brow that he couldn't see but said nothing more. The voices faded away, stolen by the breeze or by movement.

"Is that a flashlight?" Madison hissed, watching a faint glow in the same direction the voices seemed to come from. The illumination was so small and faint, she almost didn't see it. A flashlight, most likely, bobbing up and down in the night. One that was very dim or filtered to appear that way, or further away than it first appeared. Like the voices from earlier, it was difficult to place in a specific location.

"Maybe," Brash breathed.

They watched as the light grew even more faint, finally disappearing over the rim of the mountaintop.

"What's going on?" Madison dared to whisper.

"Someone was out there. Let's see if anything else happens."

They waited another fifteen minutes, but no more lights appeared. Night had fully set in. When a coyote called in the distance, Madison shivered. "Can we go now?"

"Hydrate before we start down. You'll thank me later."

Brash showed her how to use the night-vision goggles before they gathered their goods and started a slow decent down the ladder.

Madison followed close to her husband's side as they crossed the plateau. Had it been this bumpy before? She could have sworn it was flat and barren ground, but now, there were clumps of high grass and thorn bushes everywhere. Brash led the way once they started down the side of the mountain, helping her navigate the treacherous path.

More than once, they stopped as small rocks slid from beneath their feet and tumbled to the bottom, pinging against boulders on their way down. Particularly in the stillness, the base of the rocky formation sounded far, far away.

If Madison thought driving the twisting roads with a truck following her was nerve racking, it was nothing compared to the tension she felt coming down the steep, crooked footpath with darkness on her tail. The guns she and Brash carried offered zero sense of security. If they crossed paths with a rattlesnake, the fangs would be buried in her skin before either of them had time to pull their weapons. The same was true for a cougar or wild javelina, or for any attack from behind.

Having descended the worst of the mountain,

Madison heaved a sigh of relief. They weren't back at the truck yet, but here the ground spread downward at a gentle slope. They were no longer half-sliding, half-stumbling down cliffs.

"You doing okay?" Brash asked in a low voice.

"Give me a second."

After a few minutes, her breathing regulated, and her leg muscles no longer screamed for relief. Facing the inevitable, Madison steeled herself for the journey ahead. "Okay. I guess I'm as ready as I'll ever be."

Walking closely beside Brash, Madison could think of nothing but rattlesnakes and coyotes. Were they out there, just waiting to sink their fangs into the hapless couple? What if she and Brash encountered a mountain lion?

Would she feel any safer if the danger came from the person watching them? Madison mentally berated herself as her mind created wild scenarios of impending doom, each worse than the last. She kept imagining dangers from the wild, but wasn't an angry, vindictive human being the most dangerous animal of all? No, she corrected silently. The worst danger came from a desperate human being.

Madison forced her mind to focus on something other than danger.

The voices. She would think about the voices they had heard. Where had they come from? Yesterday, she and Brash heard them behind the house, down in a ravine. Tonight, they were on the opposite side of the house, most likely somewhere near the crest of Mount Perkins. The two locations were probably more than a mile apart, although judging distance had never been her strong point, and certainly not in this part of the state. Had the voices belonged to the same people?

Were these people working on the ranch? If so, had they worked for George? With him dead, who paid them? If they worked for Terrance, what were they doing on George's side of the property? Terrance didn't strike her as the sort of man who did anything out of the goodness of his heart. Her guess was that he had a nefarious reason for crossing the property line. There had to be something in it for him. Something on Dom's two hundred acres that benefited him and made it worthwhile to hire a crew to work it. Brash's theory of growing marijuana seemed plausible.

That, she reminded herself, was assuming these were ranch employees she and Brash heard. What if they weren't? That made them trespassers, didn't it? It meant they did something illegal, breaching the privacy of Dom's personal property. Trespassing in itself wasn't a heinous crime (she had done it herself a time or two), but there was potential for danger. No one wanted to be caught breaking the law.

Thinking about the voices kept her mind occupied as their feet gobbled up ground. She never thought to question Brash on how he knew where to go, but she followed with no doubt of his accuracy. All she had to do was watch where she stepped, scout occasionally for side or rear ambushes, and do it all while trying not to break her neck.

She was thinking about the light they saw when Brash suddenly stopped, tugging on her arm so that she did the same.

"What is it?" she hissed in a low whisper, swinging her attention his way.

His reply was low. "I hear something."

"What? What do you hear?"

"Shh."

Madison listened, but all she heard was the sound of the wind and a faraway call of an owl. She wrinkled her nose when she recalled the legend of *la lechuza*.

"Those trees to the left," Brash whispered. "There's probably a cavern behind them. Let's take a detour."

She wasn't exactly comforted when he traded places with her, placing himself between her and the movement. That meant he sensed trouble, and she had spent the last twenty minutes convincing herself there was no real danger out here.

"What's there?" she asked in an urgent whisper.

"Don't know." He kept his answer short, clipped, and hushed. He nudged her to turn around and retrace their steps.

Now in the lead, Madison had no idea of where she was going. Brash tugged on her arm several times to steer her in the right direction. Soon, they found a ledge that carried them up and over the cluster of trees. Madison knew to keep quiet and move as quickly as she could. She stumbled once, her foot colliding with a large clump of dried earth and sending it skittering downward. Brash pulled her up sharp and stood perfectly still, waiting to make certain nothing charged them.

By aid of a moonlit night and night-vision goggles, they once more started their descent. Madison didn't draw an easy breath until Brash led them back to the lower level where the truck was parked. He still held himself rigid, but she trusted him to get them out safely.

"How much further?" she whispered.

"Not far. You still doing okay?"

"My calves ache."

"Can you go a little further?"

That, alone, told her the danger wasn't fully passed. "What did you hear, Brash?"

"Just movement," he told her. After several more steps, he revealed some of the urgency in their push onward. "But my heat sensor picked up something."

"A deer?" She sounded hopeful, but she knew better.

"Too tall."

After those scary words, their roles reversed.

For the first time during their journey, Brash had difficulty keeping pace with her.

13

"How's that roast coming along?" Wanda asked as she came into the kitchen.

"It's done," Miss Sybil replied, "but we all know that the longer a roast cooks, the better it is."

"Smells good, that's for sure." Wanda took in a deep breath of appreciation. "How about those potatoes? They done yet?"

Granny Bert turned from the pot she tended to glare at Wanda. "Who put you in charge? You think we can't cook a meal without supervision?"

"I never said that. But the kitchen's always been my domain. It feels strange, letting someone else do the cooking."

"We all feel that way, Wanda," Miss Sybil assured her. "All four of us spent our lives cooking and cleaning and caring for our families. It's what we know."

Seeing her friend's dejected look, Granny Bert softened. "You can make a salad if you want. And some of your sweet tea."

"I made the tea this afternoon when we made

the cobbler. But a salad should go nicely with our meal."

Wanda opened the refrigerator and rummaged through the bins, looking for the makings of a salad.

"Lordy be! What kind of racket are you making over there?" Granny Bert asked.

"That wasn't me," Wanda insisted, her eyes wide with surprise.

All three women stopped in their tracks, going on full alert. Virgie was in the living room, but this racket came from the opposite direction.

Miss Sybil inched closer to her friends. "That sounded like a window breaking," she whispered.

"A tree limb, you reckon?" Wanda asked with manufactured hope.

"No trees near the back, and that came from the back of the house," Granny Bert said.

The chest of drawers still blocked the back door, so she reasoned that the office window put up the weakest defense. She held a finger to her lips to indicate silence. With only her squeaking bones to betray her position, she eased toward the kitchen door to listen.

Muffled sounds of movement came from the back room. Someone was definitely in the house.

Granny Bert turned back to her friends, motioning for them to join her. "Grab a weapon!" she whispered. She already had a rolling pin in her hands. She had foolishly left her gun in the living room. "We'll ambush them."

The three of them crowded around the

doorway. Granny Bert stood on one side with her rolling pin, Sybil stood on the other with a frying pan, and Wanda stood a few feet behind them, her large body a formidable sight even without the long tines of the roasting fork. She held it like a spear.

A shadowy figure moved into the dimly lit hallway. Darkness had fallen, and no one had thought to turn on the hall light. Shadows made the tension that much thicker. As the women waited for the person to come forward, the seconds ticked away like hours. Aging muscles, taut with apprehension, made the weapons they held feel as heavy as cannonballs.

The timing for their ambush was everything.

First, a foot appeared. As a jean-clad leg came into view, shifting its weight upon approach, Granny Bert knew the person moved with slow, deliberate stealth. When she saw the second leg move forward, she made her move. The rolling pin smacked against the person's shin, buckling their knees.

Wanda stood ready to assist as Miss Sybil swung her frying pan. The pan contacted with a solid thump!

A body fell to the ground.

Granny Bert moved to stand over the prone figure of a man not yet out of his twenties. "Good Lord, woman! I didn't say to kill him!" she chastised.

"I—I didn't know the skillet would pack such a wallop!" Miss Sybil defended herself. "I got to swinging, and the momentum just took over." Suddenly weary, her muscles gave way, and the skillet fell to the ground. She moved just in time to save her toes.

"He's not really dead, is he?" Wanda asked, her eyes round with fascinated horror.

"I don't think so. But he's out cold, at least for the time being." Granny Bert turned her head to bellow toward the living room. "Virgie! Get in here!"

Already on the way, Virgie asked, "What's all the racket in here?" She skidded to a halt when she saw her friend kneeling over a body. "Did someone faint?"

"No, Sybil near 'bout killed an intruder."

"An intruder?" Her voice came out an octave too high.

"I need you to check the office. Make certain he doesn't have a partner. You and Wanda move something in front of the window."

Virgie didn't hesitate to act. "On it."

"Sybil, find something we can use to tie up his hands and feet."

"You're sure I didn't kill him, r—right?" Worry made her voice quiver.

"You didn't kill him, but I can't say the same about us if we don't get him tied up before he comes to. Find some duct tape or something!"

The first 'something' was kitchen string, the kind used to secure packages and bind the legs of a roasting turkey. Granny Bert wound the white strand round and round the man's ankles. To keep him from hobbling away, she tied him off to the handle of the nearby bathroom door, but she was afraid the string wouldn't hold.

"Can you find me something else to tie him

with?" she asked her friend. "And bring my gun while you're at it. I left it on the coffee table. If the string doesn't slow him down, maybe staring down the end of a barrel will."

"Keep that rolling pin with you. You can knock him upside the head again if he comes to before I get back."

Granny Bert grinned at this surprising side of her easy-going friend. She never knew Sybil could be so vicious when need be.

After a mighty ruckus in the office, Virgie and Wanda returned with satisfied expressions. Wanda carried a roll of duct tape. "Taped up the window best we could," Virgie reported. "He broke it just enough to reach the lock. Opened the window and crawled through, but we pushed a filing cabinet in the way."

Wanda nodded in agreement. "It may not keep anyone else out, but it will make a holy racket when the whole thing topples over. That'll give us time to act if nothing else." She nodded to the prone body on the floor. "Want me to tie him up some more with this tape?"

"That might do it. Sybil went looking for something else besides this string."

When they were done, the man's hands were bound tightly together by a belt Sybil found. His upper arms were held close to his side, secured by triple layers of duct tape. More tape circled his knees. With his ankles tied off to the door, it was unlikely he could make a getaway.

"Whew! I'm all tuckered out!" Wanda panted.

Even though the man had a slim form, it had been no easy task for two of the older women to hold the man's chest upright while the other two wound tape around him. The most their captive had done was emit a low groan, but now that their work was done, and they stood back to critique their efforts, he stirred.

His first words were in Spanish, but they all knew the gist of his sentiments. He struggled against his restraints, squirming around on the floor with little success.

"Who are you, and why are you here?" Virgie demanded.

His eyes looked wild, but he stilled long enough to speak. "*No dañar. Agua.*" The lowly spoken word could have been an answer, could have been a request.

Ever sympathetic, Miss Sybil hurried to fetch a glass of water.

"Who are you?" Virgie repeated as the man fought against his bindings once more.

Granny Bert knew limited Spanish. "*Cómo te llamas?*"

Hearing his native language, he settled a bit. "Alberto," he answered in a heavy accent. He was the one who had broken in, yet he eyed the women around him with suspicion. "*No dañar,*" he repeated. He said another string of words, none of which they understood.

"So, you're wanting water?" It was the only word Granny Bert understood out of his rant.

"*No agua.*"

"Make up your mind! You do or do not want water?" she demanded.

"*No agua.*" He looked concerned. "*Afuera.*"

Granny Bert looked around at her friends. "Anyone know what that means? I can't decide if Sybil knocked the sense plumb out of the guy or if he's trying to tell us something. He keeps saying the same thing. What does no *dañar* mean?"

"Maybe he doesn't want a danish with his water," Wanda suggested.

Her naïve reply earned her a harsh look from both her friends. "I'm sure that's it." Virgie's voice dripped with sarcasm. "He broke into the house to say he didn't want a danish. It's tea and crumpets he's after."

Wanda sniffed away the rebuke as Sybil returned with water. He drank greedily as she held the glass to his mouth.

"For a man not wanting water, he guzzled that down lickety split," Virgie drawled.

He spoke again in Spanish, using the same word and a head motion.

"I think he's saying outside," Granny Bert deciphered.

"*Sí. Sí,*" he agreed enthusiastically.

Still, the words didn't make sense. "There's no water outside? I know it's dry this time of year, but I saw a water hydrant outside. What in tarnation is he talking about?" Granny Bert wondered.

The women made a few guesses, but none struck a chord within the bound man. Something in his manner told them he wasn't there to harm them.

He wanted—or, perhaps, didn't want— water. That seemed to be his only mission. That, and the *dañar*/danish he kept repeating.

After a few frantic head motions, another furtive attempt to free his hands, and a long string of words they didn't understand, the man seemed to have exhausted himself. He lay back panting, his dark eyes still cautious.

"He looks scared," said Wanda.

"I guess we might look a little scary," Sybil reasoned, "standing around him with our makeshift weapons. We do have him hogtied, after all." A small giggle escaped her.

Granny Bert eyed the man again. Upon closer inspection, it did seem he was more afraid of them than they were of him. He was young and thin and dressed in dirty, ragged clothing. The boots on his feet had worn soles. Bare skin peeked through a gaping hole where the stitching had come undone.

She didn't know his story. He could be homeless. He could be on the run from the law or fleeing Mexico in search of a better life. Or, he could be here to steal everything down to the door hinges in order to pay for his drug habit. Nonetheless, she felt compassion for his plight, no matter the cause.

"Sybil, see if you can find some of George's socks. Shoes, too, if you think they're anywhere near the same size as this man's."

"We're helping him?" Wanda asked in amazement. "But he broke in! How do we know he doesn't mean to do us harm?"

"I bet Virgie has her pistol on her. Am I right?"

She glanced up at the other woman, the one so like herself. Sybil had forgotten to bring Granny Bert's gun from the coffee table.

"Darn right I do," Virgie confirmed.

Granny Bert nodded with approval. "I'm not foolish enough to cut this man loose. Not yet, anyway. But I can have a bit of compassion for those less fortunate."

"I reckon everyone deserves a decent pair of shoes," Wanda agreed.

"And socks. If we can't find shoes that fit, we can at least give him socks."

Another string of Spanish words made Granny Bert suspect he understood more than he let on.

She, on the other hand, understood little of what he said. Only one word stood out. "What's this about a refrigerator?" she asked.

He nodded and went into a long spiel.

"What's he saying?" Wanda asked.

"From what I can tell, he thought there would be water in a *refrigerador* outside. I guess when he didn't find it there, he came in to get it."

"Why would there be water outside?" Wanda asked in suspicion, eying the man who called himself Alberto.

"I've heard that a lot of people in this part of the country leave water out for illegals traveling through," Virgie answered. "Keeps them from breaking in, like this fella did. Maybe George was one of those people, and now that he's dead, there's no one to leave it out."

"I remember how there used to be markings on certain houses back in the day," Wanda recalled, "that told tramps which people were willing to offer a handout."

"I think that's still happening here, either by mouth or marking," Granny Bert agreed.

"What are we going to do with him?" Sybil asked, returning with several pairs of socks and a pair of rubber boots. She dangled the boots near his feet. "Will these work?"

"Up to him. If he wants them when he goes, he can take them."

"Like Sybil asked, what are we going to do with him?" Virgie wanted to know.

"I haven't decided. I reckon we could leave him be for a while. Maybe wait to see what Brash thinks."

"He'll think we're incompetent, allowing a young whippersnapper like this one to sneak up on us!" Virgie objected.

"Who snuck up on who? I don't see any of us tied up like a Thanksgiving turkey!" Granny Bert snorted.

"True enough. Still, what if he gets loose? How can we be certain he won't hurt us?"

When Alberto jabbered some more, Wanda frowned. "I get the feeling he knows what we're saying." She maintained a safe distance between them but leaned in closer, speaking in a loud voice. "Can you understand me?"

"He's not deaf!" Granny Bert protested. "He just speaks a different language."

"I'm talking to him," Wanda sniffed. She returned to her half-shouted conversation. "Why are you here, Alberto? Did someone send you to spy on us? Hurt us? Kill us, even?"

When she held her fork tines close to his head, his eyes grew wide, and he protested.

"Stop with the danish bit!" she grumbled. "We don't have any danishes. And even if we did, we don't cater to thieves around here."

"Technically, he hasn't actually stolen anything," Sybil pointed out. "We can only get him on breaking and entering."

"What are you all of a sudden? Ms. Law and Order? The man broke in. In my book, that makes him a thief!"

"You two stop your bickering," Virgie snapped. "We need to decide what to do with him."

"We could string him up in a tree. Show the others what we do to trespassers." At Wanda's suggestion, Alberto struggled against his bindings once again.

"Stop that right now!" Granny Bert's voice was as severe as the look she pinned him with. "Tell us who sent you."

They assumed he denied being sent there.

"Did Perkins send you?" Virgie asked, eyes narrowed in suspicion.

Alberto looked at her with a blank expression.

"Did Señor Perkins tell you to come here?"

"No. No, no." He went on about the water and refrigerator outside.

"You tell your boss we ain't fooling around

here," Wanda blustered, brandishing her fork again.

"She's right," Granny Bert agreed. "You come here again, we won't need rope. You'll have bullet holes in your hide."

He knew enough English to understand the word bullet. Just in case he didn't understand the threat—which he clearly did— she pressed the toe of her shoe into his side. "You hear me, Alberto?"

"*Sí. Sí.*" They assumed the rest of his rattled words were a request not to shoot.

14

Alberto lay in the hallway for more than an hour. Granny Bert stood watch over him while her friends finished supper.

Granny Bert often came across as gruff, but it was mostly a cover for a good and generous heart. When the young man's stomach grumbled long and deep, she took mercy on him. The man was hungry. No telling when he had eaten last. She asked someone to bring her a fold-over roast beef sandwich.

"Can't you wait to eat like the rest of us?" Virgie asked with a frown.

"It's not for me. It's for him. His stomach is as empty as a politician's head."

Sybil piled a thick chunk of meat onto the bread and brought it over. Granny Bert cautiously fed him, half afraid he might bite her hand. He wolfed the half sandwich down in no time, repeating *gracias, gracias* with sincere appreciation. Wanda brought a second fold-over, and Virgie brought cheese.

"That should hold you for now," Granny Bert said when he eyed the stove in hopes of more. Granny Bert cautioned her friends from obliging. "If it's been awhile since he ate, much more will make him sick. Give him time to digest this. Maybe by the time Brash and Maddy get back, he can eat again."

Virgie looked at her watch. "What's taking them so long, anyway? They should have been back by now."

"I think I hear something." Wanda turned her head for better positioning. "Are those truck lights reflecting in the window?"

Everyone tensed, and Granny Bert warned, "Virgie, better have your gun ready. We don't need any more surprises."

They all relaxed when they heard the Cessna signature knock and Madison's voice on the other side of the front door. Alberto, however, struggled again as the newcomers entered.

Seeing the spectacle before them, Madison exclaimed, "What in the—!"

"Who's that?" Brash broke in sharply. "And what's he doing in the house?"

"I think the pertinent fact here," Granny Bert pointed out, "is that we are perfectly capable of handling an intruder."

"An intruder?" Madison chirped in alarm. "How did he get in?"

"Broke the window in the back room," Virgie supplied. "We have it patched for now, but you'll need to make it more permanent."

Brash moved closer to the bound man,

making it clear that he wasn't afraid of his thrashing legs. He placed a large, booted foot on his leg and spoke sharply to him in Spanish.

Alberto immediately stilled. After a long, suspicious glare, he answered in his native tongue. A short, terse conversation ensued.

The women peppered Brash with questions. "What's he saying?"

"Who sent him here?"

"What's he want?"

"What's all this nonsense about danishes?"

At Miss Wanda's question, Brash took his laser-like glare off Alberto and looked at her blankly. "Excuse me?"

The older woman shrugged her shoulders. "He keeps talking about *dañar*. We figured it meant danish."

"Sounds more like dinner than danish," Madison commented.

Brash corrected them all. "It means danger or harm. My Spanish is a little rusty, but I think he's saying he means you no harm." Looking back at the man's makeshift bindings, the corner of his mouth ticked upward. "Then again, maybe he's begging you not to hurt him. He does look mighty uncomfortable."

"We fed him a sandwich," Granny Bert snapped. "We weren't about to burp him and put him to bed."

"Why *is* he here, Brash?" Madison asked. "Did Perkins send him?"

"I don't think so. From what I can decipher—

again, my Spanish is Tex-Mex at best, and his is straight from Mexico— he doesn't know Perkins. He's just passing through."

"Then why does he keep talking about water in the refrigerator outside?" Granny Bert wanted to know.

After another exchange, Brash answered, "He says the *señor* is known to provide water for his kind."

Wanda hiked her roasting fork. "Criminals?"

"I think he meant illegal immigrants."

"Criminals, illegal immigrants. Both against the law," she reasoned.

Miss Sybil nibbled worriedly on her thumb. "What are we going to do with him? I gathered a few of George's old things—water boots, socks, a tee-shirt— and put some water and apples in a bag. He can take it with him when we set him free." She paused for a moment before asking, "We *are* setting him free, right?"

"He's hardly a stray puppy," Brash pointed out in a dry tone. "It's not like we can keep him."

"We could turn him over to the law," Virgie suggested.

"We could," Brash agreed, rubbing the back of his neck. "But doing so complicates matters."

The older woman was incredulous. "You're thinking of letting him go?"

"Make no mistake. I don't condone illegal aliens. It goes against everything I believe in. Our country was built on immigrants, but they should enter through the proper channels. If we want them to respect and uphold our laws, we should instill those values in them when they cross the border."

"So, we'll turn him in." Virgie's mouth was set in a stubborn line.

It was obvious the lawman was torn between duty, personal conviction, and reacting to the situation at hand. "One of the hardest parts of my job," he confessed, "is compromise. It gets under my skin every time I have to cut a deal. I'm often forced to overlook one illegal act for the sake of the greater good. It's a hard call to make, but sometimes it has to be done."

Granny Bert joined her friend in staring him down. Crossing her arms in defiance, she demanded, "What will setting this man free accomplish? What greater good are we talking about?"

"I believe there's something bigger going on here at the Perkins Ranch. I don't have proof yet, but I'd like the chance to get it. Turning this man over to the officials will only call more attention to our presence here and cut into what little time we have left to prove my suspicions." He pointed out some of the snags he foresaw. "We have no idea how long it will take for someone to get out here. We'll have to give statements. Plus, there could be repercussions for tying this man up."

"He broke in!" Wanda cried in outrage.

"We were defending ourselves!" Granny Bert insisted.

Brash warded off their protests with a splayed palm. "I understand and agree, but there's no guarantee the local authorities will feel the same. A human rights activist could turn this around on you. Instead of seeing it as detaining him until the authorities arrived, they could spin it as holding an underprivileged man hostage. I'm not saying that will happen, and I don't think it would stick, but if we have any hopes of figuring out what's going on here, we need to keep as low a profile as possible."

Madison tilted her head. "You think there's more to this than just spooking Dom out of claiming his inheritance."

"I think it's a theory worth investigating. We only have four days to find proof. Alberto's unfortunate timing complicates the matter, to say the least."

"Can he help us? Does he know what's going on here?"

Brash turned back to the bound man and asked several questions in Spanish. The women understood very little of what was said.

"According to Alberto," Brash reported, "this is a direct path from Mexico to freedom. It's a well-known route that's been used for years. The *señor's* — George's—generosity is a landmark of sorts. He claims that's all he knows."

"Do you believe him?" Virgie asked.

"Hard to say. He could be telling the truth, or he could be lying to protect himself or others."

"Do you think we can trust him if we let him go?" Granny Bert asked.

Brash studied the other man again. He had

no weapon on him. He didn't fight his restraints. He looked dejected and weary, as if already resigned to his fate. Brash could hear Alberto's stomach grumble with hunger.

"I'm willing to take my chances," Brash replied at last. "Are all you ladies on board? I'd like this to be a unanimous decision."

Miss Sybil was the first to speak. "He's barely more than a boy. I, for one, would hate to turn him in."

"I still say he's a criminal," Wanda huffed, "but I see your point."

Virgie wavered on her hard stance. "You really believe there's a greater good to be had if we set him free?"

"I can't guarantee it, but I certainly hope so," Brash said.

She sighed. "Then count me in."

Granny Bert nodded her consent. "You know I trust your judgment, son. Do what you have to do, but me and the girls want in on it."

Brash grunted out a short laugh. "Like I could keep you out of it!" He turned to his wife. "Maddy? What's your vote?"

"You know I trust you to do the best thing."

Satisfied with their answers, Brash spoke to Alberto. The bound man's eyes widened in surprise. With a vigorous nod, he thanked them profusely.

"What'd you say?" Virgie asked.

"I told him to share the word that the *señor* no longer felt so generous. I also told him we were letting him go, but he'd better not try anything foolish. And that if I ever see him again, I'll personally take him to Border Security and let them deal with him."

Wanda leaned in toward their captive. "You hear that, young man?" she shouted. "We're letting you go, but we'll have guns on you the whole time." She emulated a gun with her hand. "No funny business. *Comprende?*"

Eyes wide in fear, Alberto nodded compliance.

Brash asked the women to stand back. He took out his pocketknife and cut the tape at Alberto's knees. He left his ankles bound.

Once Alberto was on his feet, it was a long, tedious journey to the front door. The best he could do was hobble. Sybil unwound the string from the doorknob in relation to his progress. The tethering came loose before they crossed the living room, but he didn't bolt and run. (Or, in his case, hop frantically away.)

Brash cut Alberto's feet free when they reached the front door. As a silent reminder not to try anything foolish, Virgie and Wanda stood aside with their guns drawn.

After Madison cautiously opened the door, Miss Sybil set the bag of food just outside. Granny Bert tossed the clothes-stuffed boots into the yard as Brash cut Alberto's hands free and issued a stern warning in Spanish.

The women didn't know the words, but they all understood the message. For emphasis, Wanda chambered a shell into the barrel of her shotgun.

Brash pushed their intruder out the door and shut it quickly behind him. While he locked and bolted the door, the women moved to the windows. They watched Alberto scoop up the bag of food, scramble to find both boots, and take off into the night at a dead run.

By the time they ate dinner, the pot roast was so tender, it fell apart on their forks. A blackberry cobbler was the perfect ending to the meal.

"Tomorrow, I'm calling Helena, the friend who knew George," Granny Bert said. "She's been out of town but maybe she's back now and can shed some light on this mess we've gotten into."

"She never mentioned any of this to you? Nothing about the so-called curse?" Madison.

"All she said was that George wasn't like the others. He had a conscience, she said."

"That could mean anything. I'll try to get in touch with Dom, but I don't hold high hopes of that," Virgie admitted. "He's probably out fishing again."

"We have to do something," Madison agreed. "Dom said he trusted two people here. We haven't had much luck connecting with Clive Baker—"

"I asked about him again today, by the way," Brash broke in. "Still busy, busy, busy, according to Terrance."

Madison frowned. "More like stall, stall, stall. Anyway, I'll try again to reach out to the lawyer, the only other person Dom trusted. His office is in San Angelo, so it's not like I can just drop by. A round trip will kill half the day."

Wanda didn't bother stifling a big yawn. "I don't know about you folks, but I've had about as much drama and danger as I can handle. Thanks for boarding up the window all proper like," she said to Brash. "I reckon we'll all sleep better, knowing it's secure."

"I'm sure," he mumbled. He doubted he would sleep tonight, anyway. He planned to be on alert, should anyone else try to get in. He was thankful now that he had arranged an afternoon hunt with Terrance, rather than a morning hunt.

Once the dishes were done, Miss Sybil and Wanda said they were tuckered out and ready for bed. Virgie went up with them, but Granny Bert stayed behind.

"You want me to take first watch, or spell you during the night?" she asked Brash. When he looked uncertain of how to answer, she gave him an exasperated look. "We both know you won't sleep tonight, but there's no need to suffer alone. I'll do my part, same as I did the first night."

Madison frowned. "You think Alberto will come back for more food?"

"Not after these ladies tied him up and threatened him with a gun, I don't." Brash grinned, imagining how they went about it.

"Then why are you staying up?" Madison asked.

"I didn't say I was."

"Didn't say you weren't, either," Granny Bert reasoned.

Brash sent an uneasy glance toward his wife. "While Madison and I were walking back—the same time Alberto was here at the house— the heat sensor on my night-vision goggles picked up a human-sized form in a thicket. We skirted up and around the thicket, but someone followed us part of the way back to the truck."

"They what!" Madison cried. She slapped at his arm in protest. "You're just now telling me they followed us? How dare you keep that from me!"

"It would have been hard, considering I had to all but chase you back to the truck." The edges of his mouth itched with another grin.

"I knew something was wrong! I knew you were still uncomfortable. That's why I hurried. But you could have told me once we were safely inside!"

"Whoever it was didn't keep up for long. They stayed a way back, just enough to see us without us seeing them. By the time we reached the truck, the danger had passed."

"Did I do so good of a job acting like an airhead this morning that you actually think I am one? You could have trusted me with this information, you know."

Granny Bert broke in at the mention of acting. "Wait a minute. You did some more acting this morning? You're really getting the hang of this, aren't you?" The older woman couldn't have looked prouder.

"Evidently I am, because my husband now

assumes I'm too much of a dingbat to be trusted with vital information about my own safety."

"Hold on, sweetheart," he protested. "I never said—"

"That's the problem, Brash!" she snapped, refusing to let him finish his excuse. "You never said a thing. You never told me what was actually happening. So, at least tell me this. Why are you suddenly worried about it again if you felt the danger had passed?"

"In light of Alberto's unexpected visit, I think it would be prudent, don't you?"

In reply, Madison crossed her leg, bounced it a time or two, and smacked on imaginary gum. "How would I know?" she asked, fluffing her hair while she smacked. "I'm an airhead."

Granny Bert cackled with glee. "By golly, you definitely have my flare for acting!"

Brash frowned. "Don't encourage her."

They were the same words Madison normally said about her grandmother.

"She has you there, son," Granny Bert told him. "You should have been truthful with her. You men seem to think women are too fragile to handle real life, but I don't see any of you having babies, breastfeeding them, changing their diapers, and still getting dinner on the table according to your husband's work schedule. The least you can do is be honest with both of us about tonight's agenda."

"Fine. I do apologize for not telling you earlier, Madison." The look in his eyes bespoke his sincerity. "As for tonight, I'm more convinced than ever that we can't let our guard down. Something is going on here. We're being watched. Terrance Perkins wants to dictate where I hunt. Maddy found large amounts of cash in his desk drawer. It's not incriminating," he was quick to point out, "but it is suspicious. Now a man breaks into the house with all of you in it—Lord help him if he thought the four of you were helpless! — and twice now, Madison and I have heard voices floating in the air when we've been out in an open area."

Seeing a protest form on Granny Bert's lips, he was quick to pre-empt, "Something that no, we did not reveal to you. Not because you couldn't handle it, but because we're not sure where the voices were coming from or if they had a right to be there. We couldn't hear them well enough to know anything but that they were spoken in Spanish. We also have reason to believe someone is living in that deer stand on Mount Perkins. Add all of that to the fact that someone was in the thicket tonight and didn't want to be seen, and yes, I do plan to stay up tonight."

"We'll take turns." Madison's tone said the matter was settled.

Brash took her determination in stride. "First shift, middle, or last?"

Still miffed at his earlier transgression, Madison's reply was flippant. "I usually stay up late doing 'women things'—you know... laundry, birthing babies, that sort of thing—so I'll take first shift. Granny Bert is an early riser, and I figure if anything does happen, it will be in the middle of the night. I hereby elect you, the big brave man of this bunch, for middle shift." Another imaginary smack of gum accompanied her big smile.

With his signature smirk, he allowed Madison her golden moment. "*Touché*, my love."

15

The lost night's sleep turned out to be for naught. No one breached the house's security. No scream broke the stillness. No bobbing lights, or voices, or unexplained movement disturbed the moonlit night. Madison, Brash, and Granny Bert each took turns at the top of the stairs while the rest of the world slumbered.

Over breakfast—an hour later than usual, so that he could 'sleep in'—Brash asked, "What do you ladies have planned for the day?"

"I'll try to get hold of Dom. It may take all day to track him down, but I'll do my best. If service holds, I might even call that ornery husband of mine and make certain he's not gorging himself on pizza and ice cream." Virgie's words sounded indifferent, but none of them missed the note of wistfulness that crept into her voice. She clearly missed Hank.

"I only have a landline number for Helena, and she's not answering," Granny Bert said. "I guess she's still out of town."

"How do you know someone from here,

anyway?" Madison asked. "I've never thought to ask."

"Met her a time or two at conventions and workshops while I was justice of the peace. We were the only two women JPs there, so we got along well and kept in touch."

"I swear, you have connections everywhere!"

"Of course, I do," her grandmother said. "I have a solid network. How else can I know what's going on?"

Miss Sybil nodded her head in agreement, clearly proud of what she considered her best friend's accomplishments. "Like everyone always says. 'If Bertha Cessna don't know it, it ain't worth knowing.'"

"Then tell me, Miss Knows-All, Hears-All," Madison said, turning to her grandmother, "what is going on around here?"

"Well, now, I'm trying to figure it all out," she replied smartly. "I plan on calling Hugh today, that helpful rancher I met in town, and see if he can shed some light on things."

"Handy excuse," Madison smirked.

Brash broke into their squabble. "Maddy, I thought you might like to go with me today on another exploration."

His tone was casual, but his brown eyes conveyed a different message. She was pleased he treated her as an equal in his investigation. "I'd love to!"

An hour later, she wasn't so certain that was a good thing. She clearly wasn't his equal when it came to climbing and traversing this rugged land.

They had started at the ledge behind the house and walked until they found what Brash considered a suitable path to descend the steep drop-off. Madison still wasn't so certain about the 'suitable' part.

"We're going down there?" she asked dubiously, eying the deep ravine he pointed to. "By way of this steep slope? What am I supposed to do, slide down?"

"That might be rough on that cute little behind of yours," Brash said, eying her appreciatively. "I suggest we walk."

"There's no way. I'll fall and tumble my way down."

"Use that walking stick I gave you. Where is it?"

"In my backpack."

"A lot of good it does you in there," he frowned. "Turn around so I can get it."

She obliged so Brash could retrieve the folding steel rod. After extending it to its full length, he demonstrated how to use it.

Realizing how useful it could be, Madison asked, "Where was this yesterday when I needed it?"

"Just found it in George's closet this morning." He grinned.

"You're just helping yourself to all sorts of stuff, aren't you?"

"I'm simply using it while we're here. You know I'll put it all back where I found it."

"I have no doubt. Granny Bert calls you the

ultimate boy scout."

"Which I take as a compliment. Now, enough stalling. I want to get down there and look at where those voices were coming from the other day. After that, we'll go back to the mountain."

"If I survive," she moaned.

Madison had the modern version of a walking stick, but Brash had chosen a hand-carved mesquite pole for his own use. It was crooked and bent, but sturdy enough to hold even him should he start to slide.

There was no quiet way to come down the steep ravine, but Brash cautioned her against talking above a whisper. She wasn't clear on his reasoning, but she complied with his request. In her mind, it was highly unlikely the people they heard the other day were still in the same location. And even if they were, there was only a slim chance (razor-thin was more like it) that she and Brash could drop in undetected.

By the time they reached the bottom, they were quite a distance from their original destination. "We're headed over there," Brash whispered, pointing to an overhang a few hundred yards away. 'That's about where the voices were coming from."

"Lead the way," she said, readjusting her backpack. Brash had insisted they both wear them, saying you never knew what you might encounter out here. He also insisted she wear a holster and carry a pistol in case they came across a rattler.

They heard no voices today, but upon reaching their destination, they found a rock shelter eroded into the rock and protected by the overhead ledge. The shelter showed evidence of recent activity.

"Brash, this looks like some sort of camp." Madison's whisper was almost a question.

"That's exactly what it is," he agreed, keeping his voice low. "Someone's been cooking. The ashes are cold, but there was a campfire here." He motioned to a pile of small bones and a can with ragged edges, most likely opened by a knife. The label was blackened from fire and faded, but Madison thought it advertised the long-gone contents as chili. Leaves, moss, and a scrap of fabric fashioned a mattress of sorts.

"Alberto?" The question was evident in her voice.

"Maybe. This looks like more than one person, though."

"Why do you say that?"

"Those three big rocks were moved here from somewhere else. See how they're positioned around the fire? I think they're seating for at least three people. That's a bed in the back."

"Why are people living out here in the open like animals? First in a deer stand, now a cavern. I know the town of Manhattan didn't offer much in the way of housing, but this is crazy."

"I suspect it's not permanent." His face looked grim, but he offered no further explanation. After poking around the abandoned camp and finding no clues, he asked if she was ready to go.

"Where to now?"

"Just looking around, if you're up to it."

"I am."

They fanned out in a semi-circle from the makeshift camp and found two similar setups. One had seen recent use, but the other looked abandoned for quite some time.

"I know you have an idea about what's going on," Madison said as they neared the house and spoke again in normal tones. "What is it?"

"I promise I'll tell you soon. Let's check in on the ladies and head over to Mount Perkins. If we find what I think we will, it will become much clearer to us both."

Once on the mountain, Madison studied their surroundings. Mount Perkins consisted of ledges, rocky overhangs, and bands of flat ground, all winding their way up and around the peak. As far as mountains went, it wasn't extremely steep, even if her legs begged to differ. Except for a few random clusters of trees and thorny bushes, most of the surface was covered with rock. The wind, alone, was enough to beat down any grass that managed to thrive amid the dry and rocky conditions. It was almost impossible to track a footprint or find proof of recent travel.

"Good luck to us finding any clues," she mumbled.

Clueless of which direction they needed to go, Madison followed her husband's lead. Nothing struck her as familiar. In her eyes, the rocks all looked the same. It wasn't until they detoured around a cluster of yucca plants and curved to their left that Madison saw something she recognized.

The thicket of trees.

In the daylight, she realized the thicket was more brush and undergrowth than actual trees. Identifying foliage and timber had never been her strong suit, but even she recognized a hard-scrabble mix of mesquite, juniper, prickly pear, and sumac among the bushes. The trees offered just enough height to cast a bit of shade against a hot summer sun.

"Easy," Brash whispered. He motioned for her to follow him around to one side of the thicket.

Besides shade, the growth provided a natural shield for whatever laid beyond. She couldn't help but notice Brash had his pistol drawn.

Madison watched where she stepped and followed close behind. She didn't know which posed the greater danger— snakes, or the person from last night.

Using his walking stick, Brash poked the brushes in a deliberate attempt to disturb them. She didn't know if it were to scare the snakes away or to draw out their stalker, but neither thought was comforting. She put her hand on her own gun, debating on whether to unholster. Despite having a license to carry, she still wasn't comfortable handling firearms.

When nothing stirred among the bushes, Brash moved in closer and repeated the process. After a few moments, he called out a greeting. The only word Madison recognized was *amigo*.

"Stay here. Have your gun ready," he told his

wife.

"Wait! Where are you going?"

"No one answers. Could be a ploy, could be a cave entrance. I see something behind the trees."

"Be careful, Brash. Don't do anything stupid."

He offered her a lopsided smile. "I won't."

Less than a minute later, he quietly called her name.

"What? Are you okay?" she hissed.

"I'm fine, but you need to see this. You aren't going to believe it."

Madison found a place to walk that was worn free and clear of the brush. Obviously, someone used this path quite regularly. Still cautious of snakes, she slid behind the thicket and into the mouth of a small, enclosed cavern.

Just a few steps in, she realized how large the space was. There was ample headroom, even for Brash. It took only a few seconds for her to realize that someone lived here. Unlike Alberto, who claimed to be just passing through, this person obviously lived here on a permanent basis. The floors were swept clean, and there was a bed, sans a traditional mattress, set up in one corner. A colorful Mexican-style blanket made it look almost inviting. Pegs and nails had been driven into the rock walls for hanging items, and an odd assortment of items acted as furniture. Madison noted a plastic dairy crate used as a table, a log serving as a shelf, and a folding camp chair. This was one of the newer models that doubled as a rocker and came with a built-in cup holder.

"How strange is that!" she murmured, pointing to the chair. It looked out of place in such a rustic setting.

"How strange is this entire place?" her husband replied.

Only then did the full scope of their surroundings sink in. While neat and tidy at first glance, the cavity was hardly sparse. In fact, there were objects everywhere. They encompassed a wide and eclectic mix from useful to bizarre, neatly lined against the walls and stacked upon shelves fashioned from logs and tree branches.

Madison saw shoes in a wide array of styles and sizes. There were men's boots, Crocs, athletic shoes in all sizes, water boots, and even colorful children's sneakers. She saw several light blankets folded in neat stacks, a few hoodies and sweatshirts, flashlights and extra batteries, over-the-counter medications, and even some toiletries. All were lined up like a store's offerings, even though most weren't new.

Leaning more to the bizarre, strings of colorful beads, a handful of electronic gadgets *(without electricity, what good were they?)*, a piece or two of costume jewelry, and a movie poster written in Spanish hung on the opposite side of the cavern. The random collection and their arrangement made little sense to Madison, but she supposed it did to the person or persons living here.

"This looks like a thrift store in the middle of nowhere!" she said in total confusion.

Brash seemed thoughtful. "Something like

that." He walked around without disturbing anything. "Looks like only one person lives here," he noted.

"How can you tell that?"

"One bed. One chair. Only a couple of dishes, most chipped or broken. One set of clothes hanging from the peg over there. They look like something a woman might wear."

"A woman? Living out here all alone? But *why?*" Her hazel eyes were filled with consternation.

Brash had no answer, so he remained silent.

"There's more clothes over there," she pointed out.

"But they don't seem to be in use. They're neatly folded and stored away. These are hung from a peg, like they might be put on at any time."

As an amateur sleuth, she should have picked up on that fact. Madison tried to see the area from a detective's point of view.

She could deduce that the right side of the space was used for personal use. Canned goods, utilitarian baskets, a few utensils, and the chipped pottery were lined up neatly atop a log. The bed snugged into the far-right crook of the rocky space. That was the side where the poster and the beads and jewelry hung. In the middle of the space was a fire pit and cooking area. A natural hole in the overhead rock made a handy vent for smoke to escape. The rocker camp chair was pulled near the pit, angling toward the make-shift kitchen and the entrance of the cavern.

The opposite wall, she deduced, was therefore

used for something else, but she had yet to determine what that was.

Maybe I'm not cut out to be a detective, after all, she thought.

"This is all so strange," she murmured.

"I know. Very strange."

"What do we do?"

"There's not much we can do. Maybe we'll come back at another time, but I imagine that whoever lives here is watching us. She won't come out while we're here."

Before they left the cavern, Brash called out in an amicable voice. "We're not here to hurt you. We just want to talk." He repeated the words in Spanish.

Once they were outside, he called the same thing out, this time louder.

Aside from that, all they could do was hope for a response and wait.

16

Bethani was a conscientious student and rarely missed school. She was so upset the day after Myrna Lewis' accusation, however, that she made an exception.

An ace student in his own right, Trenton Torno didn't understand her urgency to leave after second period, and the two of them quarreled. It was rare for the young couple to be at odds, so by the time Bethani arrived at the deCordova Ranch, she was in tears.

"What's wrong, sweetie?" Lydia deCordova asked, taking the teen's hands into her own. "What's those tears doing on your pretty face?"

"Everything is such a mess, Grammy Lydia," she sobbed. "Myrna Lewis turned *New Beginnings* into the health department, claiming she got food poisoning there yesterday. She blamed *me* for it, too!"

"You?"

"That's not all! I've tried being nice to Miley Redmond, but it's no use. She hates me as much as her father hates my mom. She blames Mom for sending him to prison, and she takes it out on me. Anyway, somehow, she heard about the complaint and started a bunch of rumors about me at school. I was so upset—more for Aunt Genny's reputation than I was about Miley's petty lies— that I couldn't stay at school a minute longer. Now Trenton is mad at me, saying I'm putting my entire college career on the line by missing a few high school classes! He says if I start a bad habit now of putting my emotions over my studies, that I'll fall into a pattern. But I'm just too upset to sit through my classes. I can't concentrate, so I may as well not be there."

"Shh, sweetheart. Come over here and sit down, and let's have some tea. That will make you feel better, right? Let's talk this out, and it won't seem so bad. I promise." Her step-grandmother led her to the table and instructed her to sit. Moving to pour iced tea, the older woman asked, "Why does Myrna blame you? You were waitressing yesterday, weren't you? Or were they so short-handed, they put you in the kitchen?"

"Not the kitchen, thank goodness! But I had the misfortune of serving Mrs. Lewis' table, and she was nothing but trouble. Nothing I did was good enough. She was with a couple I'd never seen before, although I don't think they were a 'couple' couple." Bethani brushed away a tear as she tried to explain. "They looked more like business partners, although I have no idea how Mrs. Lewis came to be with them. The woman was very polite and pleasant, and dressed in a tailored business suit and pearls. Next to Myrna Lewis' outrageous wardrobe, she may as well have been wearing a sequined evening gown! She left me a very generous tip along with a job offer."

"A job offer?" Lydia asked, intrigued. "What kind?"

"I'm not sure. She said she owned several restaurants— or more than one, at least— and offered a very generous salary. She left a number for me to call."

"And did you?"

Bethani shook her head. "We were so busy, I didn't give it another thought, and then this happened!"

"So how did Myrna drag you into this?"

"She says I did something to her plate. I know for a fact that her eggs came out of the kitchen intact, but she called me over to complain that a yolk was busted. Later, she said I probably did it out of spite and contaminated it. Says I probably used a dirty fork or something." Bethani's lips pooched into a pretty pout. "Worst of all, I put up with her complaining throughout the entire meal for a lousy twenty-five-cent tip and a formal complaint lodged against me!"

"You know it's just Myrna being Myrna. No one ever pays her much attention anyway."

"Miley Redmond did, and she didn't waste a minute to use it against me!"

"Don't most people know Miley is a hurt, confused girl right now?" Lydia asked softly, touching Bethani's hand again. "Her mother ran off and left her. Her father turned out to be a criminal and is spending the foreseeable future behind bars. She's bitter and hurting and lashing out at anyone she can."

"But Megan and I are her favorite targets, just like Mom and Aunt Genny are Myrna Lewis' favorite targets. Why do people like them have to be so mean and spiteful?"

Lydia blew out a sigh. "I wish we knew, sweetie. If we knew what made them tick, maybe we could help them change."

"I don't think people like them ever change," the teen claimed.

"Then we have to make it a point not to allow them to change us."

"What do you mean?"

"You're always so upbeat and positive. Don't let their bitterness taint you. Be better than them."

"Easier said than done," Bethani replied glumly. "Especially when your boyfriend doesn't even understand."

"I'm sure Trenton means well. He just hates to see you so upset that you have to miss school."

"But he was so melodramatic, like missing a handful of classes is going to alter my life forever! I have a 3.9 grade average. I only miss school when I'm sick. One afternoon isn't going to kill me."

"I'm sure he'll realize he over-reacted and apologize."

"But the very worst thing of all?" Bethani admitted with a sniffle. "Miley overheard our argument! She was smirking the whole time! She'll probably go around telling everyone we're going to break up."

"Just because she says something doesn't make it true, the same way Myrna's rants don't make something true. Everything will work out, sweetie," Lydia assured her with another pat. "Just wait and see."

Across town at another kitchen table, Mary Alice Montgomery told her daughter-in-law the same thing. Both women bounced a baby in their arms.

"I don't know, Mom," Genny admitted. "This is just another chink in my armor. It seems like it's one thing after another lately. This is my second time to be turned in to the health department in just a few weeks. They could revoke my license for this!"

"Not if they don't find you at fault, which was the case last time. You never did know who called you in, did you?"

"My guess is Myrna, but I can't prove it. And I don't think she even knows Lawrence Norris." Genny kissed the top of Faith's head as she coaxed her back to sleep. "I'd blame her if I could, but I don't see a connection between the two."

Mary Alice hesitated before mentioning a recent rumor she had heard. "I don't know if there's any truth to it or not, but I heard something about a new restaurant possibly opening in town."

"A new restaurant?" Genny parroted with a puckered brow. "Who? Where?"

"I have no idea who. It may not even be true.

But I do know that someone is planning to open some sort of new business in the old dry cleaners' building."

Genny nodded and murmured, "Cutter mentioned that. But he had no idea what was going in. From what he said, it's still in its early stages."

"The rumors may not be correct. Knowing The Sisters, it could easily be conjecture."

Genny narrowed her eyes. "It makes sense, though. Maybe it's their strategy to hurt my business before they even open their doors. Stir up trouble, spread a few rumors, and cut into my customer base. The dissatisfied customers would be easy pickings for them to steal away."

"Aside from Myrna Lewis, I've never heard anyone say anything negative about *New Beginnings.* Your business has been a wonderful asset to our community, and I'm not saying that simply because my son adores you and your family. You won me over that night you catered my birthday dinner. And you know Tug was a fan of yours long before that!"

"True. My father-in-law is a big fan of my daily specials," Genny smiled.

"You had my meat-and-potatoes-loving husband eating risotto and pan-seared tilapia, long before you joined our family!" Mary Alice laughed.

"I suppose so. But not everyone is as easy to please as he is. There's always those few, like Myrna Lewis and Lawrence Norris, who have to cause a scene and make life miserable."

"Has the Norris man made any more waves?"

"Not that I'm aware of. But you know what

they say about the calm before the storm."

"I also know what they say about not borrowing troubles," Cutter's mom returned with a smile.

"*They*," Genny emphasized, "don't always know what they're talking about."

"They do in this case. You have no reason to believe that Lawrence Norris will go through with his threat, any more than you have reason to worry about Myrna's baseless claim of food poisoning. You've always had a spotless record and a perfect score with the health department. A couple of complaints don't change that fact."

"Maybe I am over-reacting..."

"You are," Mary Alice smiled again, "but it's understandable. You're a professional. It's only natural to be concerned when someone attacks you and your business."

"It just seems that the odds are against me right now. I've worked so hard to get my business to where it is today, and a few foolish, vindictive complaints can jeopardize it all."

"That's what they are, honey. Foolish and vindictive, and in no way true. Relax. This will all blow over and will soon be nothing but a vague memory. You have too many other things to think about than negative people like this Norris man and Myrna Lewis." Mary Alice looked down at the dark-haired princess she held in her arms and smiled. "These two precious babies, to start with. Now, tell me. What fascinating things have my two newest granddaughters done this week?"

Genny gladly changed the subject to her brilliant daughters. Faith had learned to coo, and Hope was blowing bubbles. She and Cutter were certain their achievements were a sure sign of genius.

But even as she rattled on about her newest loves, something in the back of her mind clouded with worry.

A storm was brewing. She was certain of it.

17

Driving back to the house at 1313 Omen, Madison could no longer contain her questions.

"What is it, Brash? What do you think is going on?"

"I think I made a mistake letting Alberto go." Regret colored his words.

"Why? Do you still think it's a marijuana operation?"

"Maybe in part, but I think there's much more going on here. I wanted to believe it was just Alberto, a lone illegal immigrant who managed to make his way across the border. But we found proof that he's only one of many. I can't prove it yet, but I suspect Terrance Perkins is smuggling immigrants through his ranch for profit."

"Wow. You got all that from just those few camps?" His hypothesis stunned her.

"Alberto said this was a well-known route that had been used for years. He also said something that I found curious. He said something about a payment."

She gasped. "The cash in Terrance's office!"

"That could be one explanation."

"I knew it was significant!" she gloated. "Why else would he have so much cash on hand?"

"I gave you several possible scenarios, but this offers another one. It fits my theory. Perkins runs a high traffic game ranch. It would be difficult to let illegals pass through his property without guests seeing them. On the other hand, the adjacent property—originally George's and now Dom's— offers the perfect solution. He can smuggle them in without putting his own business or reputation at risk."

Madison mulled over his theory. "Do you think George was in on it?"

"Hard to say. We know he was sympathetic to their plight, but that may not have stopped him from making a profit off them."

"Do you think he knew they were camping on his land?"

"I imagine that he did. More than likely, he gave them permission."

"So where does the cave we just left come into this? Why on earth is there so much *junk* in there?"

"I honestly have no idea," Brash admitted. "Hard as I try, I can't make it work into my theory at all. Along with finding proof on Perkins, that's something else we'll need to work out."

Madison continued to think over his theory as they pulled onto Omen Lane. "I thought you believed Alberto when he said he didn't know Perkins. This means he was lying the whole time."

"Maybe. Or maybe not. If Perkins is as smart as he thinks he is, he could have used a different name. The more likely scenario is that he uses one of his men to front the operation and be the bad guy."

"The Big Brute and Malcolm definitely look the part," she agreed. "I can see them being the muscle to enforce such a demand for money. I can't see anyone," she added with a bit of a snicker, "taking Terrance too seriously. He's just a little scrap of a man."

"I could have this all wrong," Brash pointed out. "Even if someone *is* smuggling in illegals, it may not be Terrance. He could be totally innocent. But my gut says he has something to hide, if only a marijuana field. He's too adamant about me hunting on his side of the fence, and I'm convinced it has nothing to do with my former days of glory or having me endorse his game hunts."

"I only disagree with the phrase '*former* days of glory.' I know for a fact that you are still in your prime as a husband, father, law officer, and all-around good man."

Pulling into the drive and putting the truck in park, Brash squirmed in his seat. "About that," he said, looking distinctly uncomfortable. "I want you to know how difficult it was for me to turn a blind eye to Alberto last night. He's an illegal immigrant. Color it how you may, but the illegal part doesn't go away. I took an oath as a lawman to uphold the laws of our land, and last night, I broke my oath by letting him go. I was uncomfortable with it before. Now I'm convinced I let emotions overrule my better judgment, and I made a colossal mistake."

Madison covered his hand with hers. "Sweetheart, we always have to second-guess the hard choices. And, yes, I know that was a hard choice for you to make. You take your commitment to the law very seriously. That's what makes you a fair and just officer and is one of the many things I love about you. But you did what you thought was right. Not because you agree with Alberto's illegal entry into our country, but because you think there's a chance to solve an even bigger crime. And if you're right about smuggling immigrants, then you're right about there being a bigger overall scheme. If this is a money-making venture for Terrance, I have no doubt he's encouraging illegals to come in by the groves, promising them safe passage for a price."

"Which makes him no better than the Coyote Cartel on the other side of the border. They do the same thing."

"So, what do we do about it?"

"For starters, I go hunting at the Perkins game ranch."

During their excursion around the property, Granny Bert had called her newfound friend Hugh. The elderly rancher was thrilled to hear from her, and even more so to set up a coffee date. His enthusiasm wavered when she mentioned bringing her granddaughter and best friend along but that he was too much of a gentleman to object.

Brash was reluctant to agree with their plans,

but he finally relented. He reasoned that the Big Brute and most of Perkins' henchmen would be occupied with him while he hunted at the ranch. No doubt they would keep a close eye on him, fearful he would snoop in places he wasn't allowed or talk to people he wasn't supposed to. The plan was for Virgie and Wanda to guard the house, while Madison, Granny Bert, and Miss Sybil drove into town.

The only place to meet for coffee was the feed store or the café side of the *So-Lo Grocery and Café*. At least the café offered cheerful, if not faded, red-checkered tablecloths.

Hugh was waiting for them when they arrived, already seated at a table for four. He stood as they approached.

"I'm mighty pleased you called, Bertha," the man said, taking his straw cowboy hat off and placing it over his chest. His smile was all for her, but he eventually acknowledged their audience. "And who have we here?"

"This is my granddaughter Maddy and my best friend Sybil. Girls, this is Hugh." No last names were mentioned, and Madison wondered if it were deliberate. Was Hugh hiding his real identity? Or was it Granny Bert who did so?

"Pleasure to meet you lovely ladies. Can I pull out your chairs for you?"

While Madison declined his gracious offer, the older two ladies were pleased to have such an attractive man fussing over them. Hugh placed Granny Bert's chair close to his own and angled it so that he could give her his full attention.

"The apple pie here is tasty if you have a hankerin' for something sweet," he said.

After ordering and exchanging the normal pleasantries, Madison decided that the old rancher was nice enough, even if he was a bit heavy-handed with the Western lingo and mannerisms. He wore a trademark red bandanna at his throat, a rawhide leather vest over his pearl-snap shirt, and scuffed boots tucked into his faded jeans.

A lot like Sticker, she noted, *except dustier.* The other difference was that Sticker Pierce, Cutter's grandfather and Granny Bert's on-again/off-again beau, had his own line of Western attire and wore monogrammed shirts.

Hugh turned out to be a good conversationalist, but Madison's mind couldn't help but wander. She eyed the people at the other tables, wondering what their connections to the town were and if any of them knew of the Perkins Curse.

With ironic timing, Hugh's voice broke into her thoughts.

"The Perkins Curse? 'Course I'm familiar with it. Everyone in these parts knows about it."

"What is it they know?" Granny Bert asked.

"That nothing good happens out there at that ranch." He drained the last bit of his coffee before elaborating, "Oh, sure, it has plenty of game animals. Brings in trickle-down revenue from the hunters, when and if they venture into town. The ranch provides room and meals, so half of the hunters never bother with the bright lights of Manhattan. But the tax dollars help pave the streets, and there's the occasional celebrity who books a hunt and wanders into town for a look around." He shrugged with indifference. "That's all fine and good for the out-of-towners, but locals don't go out there unless they have to."

Madison rejoined the conversation to ask, "What about all the people who work there?"

"That's a matter of have to," he reasoned. "Even then, they carry good-luck charms and rosary beads."

Mention of rosary beads brought to mind the beads she had seen in the cavern. Is that what those had been?

"Do you believe in the curse?" Granny Bert asked.

The man toyed with the handle of his coffee mug. "Not particularly. It all started with the legend of *La Llorona*. For the record, I don't set much store by that tale, neither, but my late wife was a firm believer. Claims she saw the ghost along the banks of the Pecos as a child. Funny thing is, there were virtually no sightings of her for a good forty years. Then all of sudden, that Reyes boy went missing, and everyone was blaming *La Llorona*. I gotta wonder where she went for the better half a century, but I reckon that's not for mere mortals to understand. So, no, I don't particularly believe in the curse, but I see no need to risk fate, neither. I avoid going out there, same as most everyone else in town."

"Did you know the Reyes that disappeared?" Madison asked.

"I knew him when I saw him. He went to school with one of my boys. Seemed like a decent sort of fellow."

"Not the type to skip town without telling anyone?"

"Not at all. He and his brother were tight. Never saw one without the other. Shoot, the whole family was tight. I can't see him just up and leaving without a trace."

Miss Sybil's dark eyes clouded with compassion. "Wasn't there an investigation into his disappearance?"

"Sure, but with nothing to go on, it didn't last a New York minute."

"What do *you* think happened to him, Hugh?" Granny Bert asked. She leaned his way slightly, looking up at him like he had all the answers to the world's problems.

Hugh looked over his shoulder to the right, then to the left. Satisfied that no one was within hearing distance, he spoke in a low voice. "There's a mean streak a mile wide in some of those Perkins men. Phillip Perkins was a fool to put those stipulations in his will. It turned his boys into a pack of hungry, greedy wolves. The kind of men that don't let nothin' stand in their way between them and what they want. If that poor boy was in their way, it couldn't have ended well for him."

His assessment stunned the three women. Madison was the first to recover. "Are—Are you suggesting—"

"I ain't suggesting nothing," he denied flatly. "I

don't know what happened, and I ain't about to stir up no ruckus by asking questions. If you know what's good for you, you'll take my advice and do the same." He abruptly got to his feet. "Bertha, I hate to run out on good company, but I have a hundred head of cattle that need tending to. Dang fools can't feed themselves, so it's up to me to put out range cubes." He tipped his hat. "Ladies, it's been a pleasure. Maybe I'll see you again before you leave town. Don't worry about the tab, it's already taken care of. Bye, now."

Without another word, the old rancher walked straight to the door and disappeared.

"Land sake's alive!" Miss Sybil exclaimed. "What was all that about? He couldn't get out of here fast enough!"

"Beats me," Granny Bert said in bewilderment. "He seemed like such a charmer, right up until he started talking about the Reyes boy."

Madison glanced out the window. "It's getting late, so that means Brash should be through hunting in about an hour. Let's order those burgers we promised and get back to the ranch."

"Maybe your man will have news that makes sense, because the one that just left sure didn't!" Granny Bert huffed.

The news Brash brought home after his hunt didn't make sense, nor was it good.

Clive Baker finally returned to the ranch.

Unfortunately, the man was dead when he did so.

"A couple of the ranch hands brought him in before I left for the blind. They shouldn't have moved the body until the officials were called," the law man in him noted, "but they claimed they were too upset to think straight. It looked like he had been dead at least a day."

"Where did they find him?" Virgie asked.

"Along the banks of the river."

"That's terrible!" Madison cried. "Do you have any idea what he died from?"

"They said they found him near a known nest of cottonmouths. I saw what could have been bite marks on his face and forearms, but considering the condition of the body, it's hard to say."

Wanda and Miss Sybil shuddered in revulsion. Virgie looked speculative.

Granny Bert was flat-out suspicious. "Rather handy, wouldn't you say? One of the two people that Dom trusted suddenly turns up dead."

Virgie agreed. "Either it's the Perkins Curse at work again, or there's something fishy going on. No pun intended," she added, "considering he was found near the river."

"If there was a known nest nearby, why would Clive go in the river at that particular location?" Madison questioned.

"That's the thing," Brash said. "I didn't see a bit of dried mud on Clive's boots or clothes. And no mud on the two men who brought him in, either. If they were anywhere near the banks of the river, they would have red mud caked on them."

Madison sat up straighter in her chair. "So, they were lying?"

"It looks like it."

"We need to find out why, Brash. Granny's friend Hugh all but accused someone on the ranch of making that Reyes man disappear back in '13. He says the Perkins men have a mean streak a mile wide and will do anything to get what they want."

Brash looked at Virgie. "Did you have any luck reaching Dom this afternoon?"

She shook her head. "Keeps going to voicemail. But I'm not giving up. I'll keep trying until he answers."

Bringing the hamburgers to the table, Granny Bert asked, "Did you find out anything else while you were over at the ranch?"

"Not really. They drove me to and from the stand. Made a big show of giving me the star treatment, but I think it was more to keep me from snooping than anything else. Told me they would push the animals my way, which, again, was their way of telling me they had their eyes on me."

"What did Terrance say about it?" asked Madison.

"I didn't have much chance to talk to him. With the men bringing in Clive's body, he had to call the JP's office and report an unattended death, then stay there until someone arrived."

"Did he? Report it, I mean?"

"I volunteered to do it for him, but he insisted it was his employee, his place. I stood there while he made the call."

"At least an autopsy will be performed," Virgie said, somewhat comforted by the thought.

Granny Bert dashed her hopes. "Not necessarily."

"What? Why not?"

"The quick version? Time and money. This is a small community and resources are probably stretched thinner than most places. If the justice of the peace determines the cause of death was likely caused by a venomous snake, and no one contests it, chances are no autopsy will be done," Granny Bert said.

"What if someone reports suspicion of foul play?"

"That would change things. Assuming, of course, that someone didn't pay to make the accusation go away. If the body went to the funeral home before the objection came in, there could always be a mishap where the body was mistakenly cremated. I'm not saying that would happen in this case, but both are possible. I've heard of such."

"Then we need to object first thing in the morning!" Virgie said.

Brash spoke up. "If Perkins has the JP or the medical examiner in his back pocket, all it will do is alert Perkins that we're on to him."

"Are you saying there's nothing we can do? We're just going to let Perkins and his men get away with possible murder?"

"I never said that," Brash objected. "But we can't just charge in, making blind accusations. We need to think this through."

"You're not going soft on us, are you, Brash?" Virgie challenged. "First, you let an illegal alien go free. Now, you don't want to turn in a suspicious death. What's all this about?"

His reply was blunt. "I'm trying to keep us safe, and alive. Dom already fears for his life. Now we're caught in the middle of it, and that makes us a target, too. I don't know for sure that Clive's death is suspicious. What I do know is that we only have a few days left to find out what's going on, and I don't like what I'm finding so far."

"What have you found? You still haven't shared your suspicions."

"At the least, I suspect there's some sort of drug activity here."

Wanda nodded. "The isolated area would make for excellent marijuana fields." When five sets of eyes turned her way, she looked appropriately innocent. "What? It's just an observation."

Accustomed to their friend's outlandish statements, Miss Sybil returned to the bigger problem. "What else, Brash? What else do you suspect?"

"I think Terrance Perkins—perhaps the whole lot of them— are smuggling in illegal aliens and charging them to cross the ranch. It's the same thing the Coyote Cartel does by charging immigrants to leave Mexico."

"They're charging them twice?" Miss Sybil was outraged. "Those poor people!"

Brash saw it differently. "Let's not forget," he reminded her. "If they came in legally, no one would charge them at all."

18

Granny Bert and her friends insisted on handling guard duty that night. Madison slept better with Brash in bed beside her all night, but she woke early in the morning and couldn't go back to sleep. She crept from the room, spoke with Miss Virgie at the top of the stairs, and went down to brood.

There was something they were missing. It always helped her to jot down the facts as she knew them and piece them together into a pattern. She pulled out her notebook and pen, thinking about what she knew.

Superstitions headed the list. Dom was superstitious, and there were plenty of superstitions floating around here at the ranch. *La Llorona. Lechuza. The Perkins Curse.* She still believed someone used those superstitions against her client to manipulate him.

The thirteenth heir. For whatever reason, Phillip Perkins had put the stipulation in his will, and now it appeared someone wanted to exploit it for their own greed. Dom was the thirteenth heir, and he believed his life was in danger because of it. He had hired her to find proof, but so far, she had nothing but speculation.

The cash. Like Brash pointed out, it wasn't a smoking gun, but it did look suspicious. It would support either of his theories: marijuana or acting as an American coyote.

Illegal immigrants. She knew they crossed the ranch. Alberto and the makeshift living quarters were proof. Brash believed the immigrants played into the overall scheme, but she wasn't convinced. Was it a profitable enough venture to kill over?

Clive Baker. He was one of two people Dom trusted, and now he was dead. Co-incidence? An effort to keep him from talking? Or was it a warning to the Louisiana cousin to stay away?

The cave. Try as she might, there was no explaining what they had found on Mount Perkins, so she didn't even try.

The Reyes disappearance. The elusive facts surrounding the case still bothered her. She couldn't quite put her finger on what it was, but something about it teased the corners of her mind.

Madison pulled out her phone, wondering if the photos she had taken of Terrance Perkins' desk might hold some clues. She scrolled through the images. Messy desktop. Files and papers stacked in a haphazard heap. Calendar pad with notations. Paper clips, pens, a mini sticky calendar from a bank. The bottom drawer with its surprise stash of cash. The built-in bookcase, its shelves filled with more photographs than books. A picture of the locked filing cabinet, and a random shot of the carpet.

She scrolled backward, studying each photo as she went. When she zoomed in, she saw that while many of his photos were with hunters and their trophy kills, some were of him and what appeared to be Hispanic businessmen. In one photo, they stood in front of an impressive building with a sign written in Spanish.

Hadn't she just seen that logo? She enlarged the photo taken of his pencil drawer. *Yes.* The logo on the building matched the logo on the mini calendar given out by a bank. Some symbols were universal.

Her mind raced with possibilities, but she reined in her excitement. *Proves nothing, Madison,* she reminded herself. *So what if he does business with a bank in Mexico?*

While examining the photo of the bottom drawer, she noticed for the first time that one of her shots included most of the entire drawer, and not just the folder with the cash. While the money folder was bulky and worn, the ones behind it were neat and trim, each labeled with the year only. Starting with the current year, they followed in descending order. If there was a folder after 2013, it wasn't included in the shot.

Probably year-end financial reports, she surmised, *behind lock and key.*

She studied the photo of his calendar pad. Today was Saturday and had a carelessly drawn circle around it. The loop wasn't quite complete. *Come to think of it, none of the circles around the dates meet, except for Monday and Tuesday.* She snickered aloud. *Good work, Terry. After a half-dozen tries, you can now draw a complete circle!*

The snide thought made her feel better, even if the man never heard the insult.

She wondered what the two vertical marks meant on Monday's date. Did they signify the numeral two? A count of some kind? Random doodles?

No matter, she thought with a shrug of her shoulders. *Not much here to use.*

"What has you so engrossed this time of morning?" Brash's voice asked from the doorway.

Startled, Madison's hand came to her chest. "What are you doing up? I was trying not to wake you."

"I reached for you, and you weren't there. I came to check on you. Are you okay?"

"I couldn't sleep. I keep thinking there's something we aren't seeing."

"I know the feeling. But there's another possibility we need to consider." He settled heavily into the kitchen chair, his mood equally weighted.

"And what is that?"

"That maybe there's nothing to see. Any so-called danger may all be a figment of Dom's imagination. The man is admittedly superstitious. Maybe he's blown everything out of proportion."

She gave her husband a level look. "Do you really believe that?"

"No, but we can't rule it out."

"Then why is someone watching us? We can

feel their eyes on us. Even if we were wrong about that, there's no denying the black truck tailed me to and from town. Someone followed us on that mountainside. You saw the proof on your night-vision goggles. Those things aren't imagined."

"No, but they also aren't proof of any wrongdoing. We're strangers in town. Staying on private property that, for all the locals know, we have no right to be on."

Madison crossed her arms over her waist. "Nice try, but we both know that's a bunch of malarkey."

"The first rule of conducting a thorough investigation is to keep an open mind."

"So noted," she said dryly. "And in answer to your question, I'm making myself notes and going through the photos from Perkins' desk."

"Find anything of interest?"

"Not really," she admitted. "I know he's a slob and not very good at drawing circles, but that's about it."

Not following her meaning, Brash's brows drew together. "Circles?"

She showed him the calendar and how the circles didn't align. "He finally got it right, though, after... one, two..." she counted aloud, "...six tries. Lucky number seven was a winner!"

"Let me see that."

She left him her phone as she got up and moved to the coffee pot. "I can't promise my coffee will be as good Granny Bert's, but I need some caffeine and am desperate enough to make it myself."

He made a noncommittal reply, engrossed with the image on her phone. After a moment, he pulled out his own phone, typed something onto the screen, and compared the two.

"Hey, Maddy? Look at this."

She came to stand over his shoulder. "What am I looking at?"

"These are the phases of the moon. Monday night will be a full moon. Full moon, full circle."

Madison compared the two images from different angles. "Huh," she finally said. "That's strange. What do you think it means?"

"That Terrance believes in astrology? Maybe he plants food plots according to the phases of the moon."

"Maybe," she said, sounding doubtful. "I'm still going with strange."

"Like the man himself."

"Exactly." She dropped a kiss onto Brash's forehead before returning to the coffee pot.

He continued to look through her pictures. "What year did you say that Reyes fella went missing?"

"October thirteenth of 2013. I remember because of the thirteen-thirteen connection. Rather superstitious, don't you think?"

"Superstitious, or suspicious?" he grunted.

"Hugh, Granny Bert's rancher friend, said it was the first time *La Llorona* had been sighted in forty years. Apparently, she came back with a vengeance."

"Apparently so."

"Is that significant?" she asked, noting his pensive expression.

"Just thinking. Trying to make sense of it all."

Madison's mouth tugged into an 'I hate to tell you this' expression as she said, "I'm not sure there's any making sense of a ghost sighting."

"You have a point."

She spooned healthy portions of coffee grounds into the filter basket, slid it into place, and turned on the brewer. "Brash? I keep thinking about that crazy cave. I can't come up with a single explanation of why all that stuff is out there! I can't stop thinking about it."

"To be honest, neither can I. I can make almost everything else we've found fit into some sort of scenario, but that cave just doesn't fit at all."

"I think we need to go back. We'll camp out all day if we have to. Sooner or later, the person living there has to show up."

"That means leaving the ladies alone here at the house."

"I think they proved they can take care of themselves."

"Fair enough. But you realize we could be in for a very long day," he warned.

Up to the challenge, she replied, "I'll pack us a lunch."

After breakfast, Madison and Brash prepared for a day on the mountain. With Granny Bert and Virgie in the cab, they rode lying down in the bed of the truck to avoid being seen. Virgie drove to the spot Brash had previously parked, and the two elderly women got out, carrying baskets.

The ladies made a show of foraging for prickly pear. They argued over the best way to pluck it from the plant without coming away with a handful of needles. Stomping and romping across the rocky ledges, they discussed recipes and the best way to prepare *nopales.*

While the two 'actresses' put on their show, Brash and Madison crept from the truck and snuck their way into the brush. By the time the truck rumbled back down, they were stationed near the mouth of the shelter.

Brash slipped behind the stand of trees and into the cavern, once again finding it empty. He motioned for his wife to follow.

"Someone was here this morning," he whispered. "I smell coffee, and the ashes are still warm."

"Maybe she'll be back soon."

They settled in for the wait, staying at the back of the cave in the shadows and making as little noise as possible. Madison nodded off a few times, slightly bored, and tired after waking so early.

It was near noon when they heard sounds of rustling. Brash gently shook Maddy to wake her. He held up a finger in caution and nodded to the disturbance outside.

Someone slipped quietly into the cave, their face hidden in the shadows. A man's voice called out softly, "Vali? *Estás aquí?*" When he received no answer, he asked again, "Vali, are you here?"

He stepped deeper into the shadows, unknowingly coming close to where Brash and Madison waited. Only then did Brash see his face.

"Hello, Alberto," he said quietly.

The younger man jumped back, frightened by the voice and the swiftness with which Brash came to his feet. When he would have run, Brash stopped him.

His hold on Alberto's arm was loose but firm. "So. You do speak English."

Alberto babbled a denial in his native language.

"Speak English," Brash ordered, "or we go to the authorities right now!"

"*Sí.* Yes," he relented. "Some English."

"Why are you here?"

Alberto darted his eyes around the space, looking for a way to escape.

"Tell me, Alberto," Brash barked. "Why are you here, and who is Vali?"

"She—She lives here. I come see her."

"Why? How do you know her?"

"Everyone know Vali. She *angel de la misericordia.* Angel of mercy."

"How is that?" Alberto looked uncertain of his meaning, so Brash rephrased. "Why do you call her an angel of mercy?"

"She help people." He motioned toward the mishmash of goods on one side of the cave.

Having scrambled to her feet behind them, Madison stepped forward. "Is that what all this is? Help?"

"*Sí.* She help."

"Who does she help, Alberto?"

Her tone was softer than her husband's had been. Alberto, still clearly frightened of Brash, darted his dark eyes toward him.

"It's okay, Alberto," Madison urged. "We mean you no harm. We want to understand what all this is." Her hand panned toward what she still described as a mountainside thrift store.

Brash dropped his hold on the younger man's arm. He held both palms up to show he posed no danger, even though they both knew that wasn't so. Brash could easily catch and detain Alberto if he attempted to get away.

Alberto opened his mouth to speak, but the voice they heard was hoarse and crackled with age. The sharply spoken Spanish words startled them all.

All eyes turned to the newcomer. For one crazy moment, Madison wondered if she were staring at *La Llorona,* herself. The old woman before them was small and bent, with skin that resembled used sandpaper and a stature that barely reached five feet. A mane of solid white hung past her waist, thick and wild, like an evil storybook witch. Feeling very much like Hansel and Gretel, Madison edged closer to her husband.

Alberto replied to the woman's bark, his explanation including hand gestures. When the old woman swung her gaze to the couple, Madison attempted a weak smile and a timid wave.

Speaking from one side of the mouth, Madison hissed, "What did they say?"

Brash had no chance to reply. The old woman was as good at interrupting as Granny Bert.

"I ask why you here!" The woman spoke in heavily accented English.

"We, uh, found this place yesterday," Madison offered.

"I know. Why you come back?"

Ever the gentleman, Brash stepped forward to offer his hand. "My name is Brash deCordova. This is my wife Madison."

The woman tried looking indifferent, but even she wasn't immune to his easy charm. She accepted his handshake. "Valencia." She offered no surname.

Madison offered her hand, as well. "Alberto says you're known as the angel of mercy."

"Alberto talks," she said brusquely, but there was real affection in her voice.

"In English, so it seems." With his signature smirk, Brash looked at the other man.

Under such scrutiny, Alberto squirmed. "I did not know if you *amigo* or no."

"And now?"

The younger man shrugged his thin shoulders.

Valencia slapped his arm with the back of her hand. "He let you go! He close enough to one," she chided. She turned and addressed Brash bluntly. "Why did you?"

"Why did I what?"

"Let him go?"

"He posed no danger to us."

"Why the women tie him up?"

"He broke a window and came into the house. He frightened them."

Valencia looked amused. "Frightened she-warriors?"

Madison smiled at the compliment. "They'll be pleased to know you called them warriors."

"They feed Alberto. True warriors show strength, and softness."

Madison glanced down at the young man's feet, recognizing the rubber boots he wore.

"Would you talk with us, *Señora* Valencia?" Brash asked.

"I am called Vali," she corrected him.

"We'd like to ask you some questions. May we sit?"

She spoke in her native tongue to Alberto, who hurried to bring extra seating. He rolled two large stumps toward the fire pit and turned them upright. Brash motioned for Vali to take the rocker and Madison one of the stumps. He sat on the other as Alberto plopped cross-legged onto the dirt floor.

Without preamble—perhaps unaccustomed to visitors, or simply her way— Vali started the conversation with a barked, "What?"

Brash shot his wife a look. "Granny Bert would like her," he said with a half smile.

Alberto explained the dynamics of his previous captors to Vali. "She gave me roast beef. The leader of she-warriors."

Vali nodded her wild white hair in approval.

Clearing his throat, Brash broached his first question with caution. "How did you come to live here?"

"In wild, you mean?" Her eyes blazed. She mistook his question as an insult.

"On George Perkins' land."

"Ah, Jorge." She used the Hispanic pronunciation of his name. "He was good man."

"You knew him, then?" Madison asked. She sensed that not only had Vali known him, but that she had been fond of him.

"*Sí.*" Vali's gnarled fingers ran along the arm of her folding rocker. "The last thing he brought me."

"I have that model myself," Brash said with approval.

She rewarded him with a minuscule smile.

Madison looked around the odd mix of cluster that, somehow, wasn't cluttered at all. "You have an interesting home here."

The old woman shrugged. "It suits me."

"Do you live here, too, Alberto?"

Despite Madison's friendly question, his answer was cautious. "No. I live... somewhere else."

"You have a good setup here," Brash told their hostess. "Good cover. Natural ventilation. The stone should keep it cool in the summertime. Are you close to a water source?"

"Close enough," the woman acknowledged. Again, she shrugged. "I have what I need."

Conversing with her wasn't easy. She answered easily enough but offered nothing extra. She made them work for every morsel.

"Tell me about your collections," Madison said. She didn't indicate which one she referred to.

"Gifts." Her tone was somewhat defensive.

Did she think they accused her of stealing? Madison was quick to dispel that notion. "That poster caught my eye. I think I recognize the movie. I watched it with Granny Bert when I was young. Is that a true souvenir, or a gift?"

"I don't know that word. Sou—?"

"Souvenir. It means keepsake. I thought maybe you saw the movie in Mexico and brought the poster with you to remember it."

"No movies," she said, a touch of sadness in her voice. "A gift."

Finding this more difficult than she originally imagined, Madison tried again. "Alberto says you help people?" This time, she clearly indicated the collection of neatly displayed items.

"If they need it."

Wow! Make me pull teeth, why don't you! Madison groused to herself.

She gave it another try. "Are these people ranch hands?" she asked. "Is that how you know them?"

"They are workers, yes."

Noting that she didn't directly answer the question, Brash took over. His tone inspired confidence.

"We aren't here to turn you in, Vali. We just want to know what's going on. We've noticed some…" he searched for the right word, not knowing her part in all this, "…strange happenings at the ranch."

She gave him the eagle-eye. "You friend of

Jorge?"

"I'm afraid we never knew him," Brash admitted. "But we're a friend of his nephew Dom." It was a little white lie, seeing as they had never actually met the man. It eased his conscience to think of it as a royal *we*, meaning Virgie.

"He owns the house now," the older woman acknowledged.

"Oh, so you've heard of him!" Madison was pleased. If Vali knew about Dom, she and George had probably been closer than she first thought.

"Jorge liked him *mucho*. Always talked." Her finger movement explained more, indicating that George had often spoken of his nephew.

"Dom asked us to come here," Brash explained. "He was worried that something bad was happening here at the ranch."

Vali shook her head. "Not here," she denied, motioning to their immediate area. She pointed north, toward the land on the other side of the high game fence. "There."

Finally! Thrilled to have an opening, Brash hid his excitement with a calm nod. The gesture suggested he had expected such a reply.

In truth, it was more than he had hoped for.

"You know what Perkins is up to?" he asked.

"I know."

Her lips were as tight as her answer. He was frustrated, until Alberto spoke up.

"I watch." The young man tapped beside his eye, and then his ear. "I hear things. I help the angel."

A thought occurred to Brash. "Are you the one

who's been watching us, Alberto? Do you live in the deer stand?"?

"It's the best lookout," he boasted. "I see all Pecos Valley."

"We thought it was Perkins up there," Brash admitted. "It was you?"

"*Sí.*"

"Why?"

"To be sure."

"To be sure of what?"

"You friendly. Not one of *them.*" He described the Perkins with disdain.

"I promise you, we're not one of them. We thought it was Perkins, wanting to hurt us."

"I no let," Alberto assured him. He didn't explain how he, the man ambushed and bound by four senior citizens, would have stopped it.

"What else are you watching, Alberto?"

"The full moon. Movement. *La Llorona.*"

His answer offered little explanation. Madison glanced at Vali, who listened without comment. "This helps you?" she asked the old woman.

"Alberto big help," Vali assured her. Her first real smile broke through as she looked at the young man. Several of her front teeth were worn down to mere stubs or missing altogether.

"Can you tell us what you do, Vali? What does Alberto help you with?"

Vali and Alberto exchanged a cautious look. Both were reluctant to trust the outsiders.

"We can't help you, Vali," Madison said softly, "unless we know what you do. Dom asked me to find out about the danger."

"I am old woman," she said.

They thought that was her only explanation until, with a faraway look in her eyes, she offered more.

"All my life, I hear what a grand place America is. How much freedom. How much money. How much future. All my life, my family save. We do without. We save more. Years pass, and we have enough money to come. Then I get here, and they tell me I too old. Too weak. I hurt foot, so they leave me behind to die."

Madison's heart ached, hearing the raw pain in Vali's voice. It spoke of disillusion and broken dreams.

"But Perkins wrong." She tapped on her chest. "I strong. I stubborn. I survive. I find way to work against him. Way to help more like me."

"Illegal immigrants?" Madison asked in a gentle tone.

She glanced uneasily at Brash but gave an honest answer. "*Sí.* Dreamers, like me. Hard workers, like me. Good people."

"Like you."

Vali was honest enough to shrug. "Maybe, maybe not. My heart has turned hard. I seek revenge."

Brash looked at the rows of neatly aligned goods. Some were new, some gently used, some on the verge of extinction. All had a worthy place on the makeshift shelves. All had value to someone.

"Is that what revenge looks like?" A smile

twitched on his lips.

She pretended indifference. "Sometimes."

"I still don't understand, Vali. How does all of this—" Madison waved to the odd assortment— "help you get revenge on Perkins?"

"Free for them. Cost him money."

"Perkins pays for this?"

"No!" Her laugh was short and callous. "For every person I help, he lose money."

Seeing the confusion on their faces, Alberto helped to explain. "The angel no take money. She take what people can give. Extra blanket. Spare shoes. Can of food. They take with them what they need. Fresh water. Medicine. Clothes."

"Like a lending library," Madison realized.

Having no idea what a lending library was, Alberto said, "Perkins, he not nice. He take much more."

"He charges them money." Brash's grim words weren't a question. "Their life savings."

"Other things, too." Alberto pushed off a borrowed boot. Peeling back one of George's socks, he displayed his foot. Two toes were missing.

Madison was horrified. "He did that to you?" she shrieked, jumping to her feet. If Terrance Perkins were here now, she would cut off more than his toes.

Brash gently pulled her back down. Alberto was telling his story.

"I was boy. Sickly, so they left me behind. They marked my weakness." He waved his foot again before hiding the horrific evidence beneath a sock.

"I—I can't believe someone would do that to a boy!"

"They left him to die, like they did me," Vali spoke quietly. "I found him and helped him heal."

"She was my angel of mercy," Alberto said, emotion glistening in his dark eyes.

Madison was stunned. "You healed him by yourself? Without a doctor? That—That's amazing!"

"It take long time. But he grow stronger. Alberto good boy, grow to good man."

"It was just the two of you, out here alone." Madison was still in disbelief.

"Not alone. We have us." She waved her finger between Alberto and herself. It translated to 'we have each other.'

"How did you survive? How did you eat?"

"Land feed us. River feed us." She made a gesture of nonchalance. "Jorge feed us."

"But you lived here, in the cave."

Alberto was quick to point out, "Only while *niño*. I move when old enough." He was proud of his independence and the ability to survive on his own.

"We make team," Vali told her. "Team against Perkins. Fight him together. Revenge make us strong."

Madison's eyes shone with admiration. "Revenge? Or justice?"

"Sometimes, two things make one thing."

Alberto nodded in vigorous agreement. "Revenge to Perkins, justice to us."

"We want to help," Brash told the brave survivors. "We want justice for you both. We want to make Perkins pay, but we need to know exactly what he's doing."

After some hesitation, Vali nodded. "Two nights."

"Tonight? What about tonight?"

"No. In two nights. Full moon. *La Llorona* come."

Brash and Madison exchanged a confused look. Clearly, their hosts were believers in the old superstition. But how did that play into Perkins' downfall? Did they hope the ghost would somehow curse him?

"You've seen *La Llorona*?" Brash asked cautiously. If they were true believers in the legend, he didn't want to say anything to offend them. Insulting them at this point would be detrimental.

Alberto nodded. "We both see."

"How do you know she'll come during the full moon?" Madison asked.

With a calm and certain demeanor, Vali's assured her with a mystic, "I know."

The same thought ran through both her guests' heads. *That's no help. We can't depend on a ghost to fight Perkins.*

Trying hard not to sound judgmental, Brash pushed for more information. "We want to help, but we can't unless we know more. We need to know what we're up against."

Vali was uncertain of his meaning. Like Alberto, some American phrases were not familiar to her.

"We need to know everything," he amended.

"We need to know what Perkins is doing before we can know how to stop him."

The old woman thought over his request. After a long moment, she said, "You will bring the she-warriors, yes?"

Brash sensed it was a requirement, not a request.

Lord help us all, he thought silently.

Against his better judgment, he heard himself agreeing, "Yes."

She nodded in satisfaction, her wild white hair like a cloud. "Perkins is evil," Vali said. "Listen, and I tell you how much so."

19

The Sisters, Texas

Genny called a staff meeting after *New Beginnings* closed on Saturday. Thanks to his parents watching the girls, Cutter was there to support his wife.

Even though they didn't work at the café, Megan and Blake were invited to attend. The Montgomerys insisted they were a part of the team the same as everyone else. Without Megan babysitting, Genny's time at the café would be limited. Without Blake, the flowerbeds would suffer and morale at the café would dip. Not only did the handsome teen keep everyone entertained with his lively stories, but his presence boosted the patronage of teenage girls.

"Thank you all for coming tonight," Genny said, taking Cutter's hand for courage. "We'll get straight to the point. *New Beginnings* is under attack, and we need your help to fight this."

"I don't know what you need," Thelma interrupted her, "but count me in! This is the best job

I've ever had. The best bosses, too."

Genny smiled. "Thank you, Thelma."

"Me, too," Dierra said.

"Who's doing this?" Joey, one of the workers in the back of the house, wanted to know. "Me and my buddies can rough them up."

"We can't do that, but there is plenty else we can do," Genny assured him. "First, we need to find out where the threat is coming from."

"Besides Myrna Lewis, you mean?" someone asked. "That old busybody is nothing but trouble!"

"I agree, but I don't think we can blame this solely on Myrna. I feel sure she has help."

"That, or she's helping someone else," another person suggested.

"Good point, Ann. Any ideas who?"

The woman looked uncomfortable. "I didn't want to say anything before," she admitted, sliding her eyes away from her boss, "but I saw her over at the old dry cleaners' building. She was with that couple eating with her the other day."

"The nice lady in the pearls?" Bethani asked. She was somehow surprised, even though she knew they had come in together.

"That's the one," Ann nodded.

"Does anyone know what kind of business is going in?" Thelma asked. "They were painting the name on the windows when I came by. It said Fresh Star, but I think they hadn't painted the last 't' yet."

"Fresh Start?" asked Trenessa, Genny's assistant and acting manager.

"I would imagine, but I don't know for sure."

Cutter spoke up. "Any reason you think that, Ann? Are you familiar with the name?"

"No, but it would make a good name for a café. Especially one in competition with *New Beginnings*," she reasoned. "If people can't remember the exact name, they may Google something similar."

"I heard there was a new place coming in," someone murmured.

"Me, too," agreed a co-worker.

"Make that three."

"I heard the same thing."

Genny missed some of the exchange, thinking over what Ann said. She had a point. Locals knew exactly where *New Beginnings* was, but visitors weren't as familiar with the two towns that comprised The Sisters. The café still enjoyed trickle-down business from *Home Again's* heyday, but it *had* been two years. Viewers may have forgotten the exact name of the café. An internet search for anything close—Fresh Start, Fresh Beginnings, New Tastes— could lead to someone mistaking an upstart café to her tried and true favorite. She doubted the error would cause significant damage, but added to the recent chain of events, she couldn't rule out the possibility.

Fighting off a sudden surge of panic, Genny tried presenting a calm demeanor to her team. She hoped her smile was convincing. "I think there's enough business to support another restaurant in town, don't you? We have *New Beginnings*, *Montelongo's Mexican Restaurant,* the donut shop, delis in our three convenience stores, and *Reno's*

Traveling Kitchen. I hope this *Fresh Start* specializes in seafood!" She rubbed her hands together in pretend excitement. In truth, she was trying to hide their slight tremble.

"No one can beat your tilapia, Miss Genny," Dierra insisted. "I was a fan of it long before I started working here. Your special shrimp and grits, too."

"Thank you, Dierra."

Other employees pitched in with their own form of support, raving about one dish or another.

Cutter pulled his wife to his side, dropping a kiss on her blond hair. "Everyone knows how much I love your apple turnovers. They were half the reason I accepted your marriage proposal!" he teased.

His wife couldn't help the stain creeping into her cheeks. The fact was, she *had* proposed to him. Publicly. But only after he made it crystal clear that he intended to marry her and grow old at her side. Cutter had never tried hiding the fact that he was hopelessly and utterly in love with the restaurateur. She had hurt him by ignoring his first declarations of love and dreams for the future, so she had made amends by publicly acknowledging that the feelings were mutual.

Two years after their infamous engagement, hearts were still broken over the fact that Cutter Montgomery was taken.

Sensing her embarrassment, he cuddled her close. "Everyone also knows," he added, "the other reason is that I can't live without you."

"Nice save, Mr. Gennecut," she said dryly,

poking him in the side with her elbow. Gennecut was the 'power couple' hashtag they were given during the reality show. Dismissing his foolishness, she addressed her employees. "So, back to business. It makes sense that a rival start-up would want to stir up trouble for us, but we can't rule out other possibilities. Any other thoughts on that?"

"Myrna Lewis," someone snickered.

"What about that Norris guy? He has it in for us, too." This suggestion came from someone else working in the kitchen. It pleased Genny to know that everyone, not just those seen out front, felt like a part of their team.

"I agree. I think it's a definite possibility," she said. "Anyone else? With our two little new bundles of joy, I'm not out and about the way I once was. I don't hear all the latest gossip. I'm depending on all of you to be my eyes and ears. Please, let me know if you've seen or heard anything. Anything at all that may be helpful."

There were a few comments from around the room, very few which were pertinent to this situation.

"The junior class is looking for somewhere to hold their prom. Maybe they're hoping you'll cut them a good deal if your business falls off."

Blake perked up at mention of a venue. "The Drama Club needs a place for our New Year's Eve Masquerade Ball. Has anyone called you about it?"

"Yes, but I'm afraid we aren't taking party reservations this year."

"Not even for your favorite nephew?" he

asked hopefully. "We had a place booked in Riverton, but they just canceled on us."

"Sorry, Blake. We've already turned down two other requests."

"I don't know about party reservations," someone else pitched in, "but I heard there's some big event coming this summer. A political rally of some kind. Maybe they're the ones wanting a discount."

"We don't do political events," Cutter said firmly.

"I don't think it's someone trying to get a good deal on a booking," Genny added. "Why ruin a business' reputation, and then expect your guests to be excited about coming there? I think it's something else."

Everyone had a different opinion.

"I still say it's Myrna Lewis."

"I think it's a new business that's coming in. This Fresh Start seems like a good culprit."

"Could be one of the existing businesses, trying to beef up their own sales," someone else argued.

"Nah, it's Myrna. Don't put anything past her."

"Yeah, remember that big stink she put up against Chief deCordova, trying to take his job away from him? She knows y'all are tight with the deCordovas. This is just another way to get even with all of you."

"You should have seen her picking on poor Bethani that day!" Thelma agreed. "She's nothing but a menace. A spiteful, bitter old menace!"

"I agree, but does she even know that Norris guy? He's not a local," Trenessa pointed out. "It seems like a big coincidence that all of this is happening at once. As mean and ornery as Myrna Lewis is, she tends to think only of herself. I'm not sure she could coordinate something on a large scale."

"Maybe it's a jilted ex-boyfriend," someone else suggested.

"Doubtful," Genny frowned, thinking of the disaster one ex had created.

"What about a jilted girlfriend? Someone said they saw Shiloh Dawn Nedbalek in town last week."

Shiloh Dawn was a former employee and someone she considered a friend. The girl had been desperately in love with Cutter, but he was already falling for Genny. The former server left town before they officially became an item, but she would have had to live under a rock to miss their romance as it played out on national television. To Genny's knowledge, they had all parted on amicable terms. She couldn't fathom the girl having a vendetta against either of them after all this time.

"Really? I'd love to see her again," Genny said, meaning it.

"What about a disgruntled employee? There was that one guy who washed dishes for like two hours and walked out in the middle of his shift. Maybe he's trying to get even."

"That was a long time ago. Surely he's over that by now!"

Hearing only a handful of other suggestions,

Cutter asked everyone to stay alert to any rumors and to report them to Trenessa, Genny, or himself. He stressed that no one should engage in spreading rumors or false accusations.

After a pep talk to boost morale and thank everyone for their loyalty and support, Genny closed their meeting and sent them all home. She promised their paychecks would reflect the extra hour spent in the meeting.

"I think that went well, don't you?" she said, taking a seat at the table where Bethani, Blake, and Megan still lingered.

"I don't think you need to worry, Aunt Genny," Blake assured her. "Everyone loves you."

"Obviously, someone doesn't," she argued.

"Aw, don't sweat it. It will blow over."

"I agree with most of the others. I think it's Myrna Lewis," Bethani insisted. "Like Thelma said, it's directed at me and Mom as much as it is at you. You know the old bat hates all of us."

"I'm not sure there's many people she does like, to be honest," Cutter said.

Bethani nodded. "But that sort of surprises me about Ms. Rowland."

"Who's that?"

Bethani shot her 'aunt' a guilty look. "Uhm, that's the lady who came in with Mrs. Lewis. Her name is Anastasia Rowland."

"Anastasia Rowland?"

Seeing Genny's surprise, Cutter asked, "You know the name?"

"Of course. She owns several cafés and bistros

in the greater Houston area, including down along the coast. Several of them specialize in breakfast."

"Like Fresh Start?" Megan guessed. "A double meaning, you think?"

"Possibly."

"Aunt Genny, I think there's something you should know," Bethani confessed. "I really haven't given it much thought—we were so busy that day, and now all this mess! — but Ms. Rowland offered me a job."

"A job? Where?"

"That's the thing. I don't know. She left me a note on a napkin, along with her phone number and a generous tip. I never dreamed it might be here in The Sisters, working for a rival café! If I had known that, I wouldn't have been so nice to her!"

She relayed what she remembered about their encounter. She recalled Myrna had grumbled something about poor management and needing a restaurant that knew about true service.

"I'm sorry I didn't tell you 'til now. I never gave it another thought."

"And don't do so now," Genny told her, patting her hand. "It's fine. And if Anastasia is putting in a restaurant here, I wish her well. I met her once at a culinary event, and she seemed nice."

"I thought so, too. But if she's in cahoots with Myrna Lewis..."

"Then she needs our prayers!" Blake quipped, lightening the mood. "Hey. Is there anything left to eat in the kitchen? I'm hungry."

"Didn't you eat at the ranch before you came?"

his twin asked.

"Yeah." He spread his hands with a gesture of inquiry. "What's your point?"

"Come on, Mr. Endless Pit. If Aunt Genny doesn't mind, I'll find you something to eat and let you clean up your mess before we go."

"Help yourself," Genny replied. "And kids? Thanks for being here tonight. I need my family around me right now." Her brave smile faltered just a bit.

"We love you, Aunt Genny," Bethani assured her.

"Of course we're here for you!" Megan agreed.

"I'd be here even without the food," Blake insisted. He flashed a charming smile. "But an extra slice of pie sure doesn't hurt."

Watching them head for the kitchen, Genny shook her head with an affectionate smile. "That boy."

'They're all three good kids," Cutter agreed. He leaned over to give her a kiss. "Don't worry, Genny. We've got this."

"Can you promise me that? In writing? Because right now, I'm not so sure."

"I am. We'll get through this just fine. It will make us stronger for the next obstacle that gets thrown our way."

"Hey, let me get through one crisis at a time, please."

'This isn't a crisis, darlin'. It's a bump in the road. Nowhere near big enough to knock us off course."

"I hope so. Because if Myrna Lewis *is* behind this, she's known for her steamrolling techniques. With her, a bump becomes a mountain."

"Sort of like her figure?" he cracked.

"You're bad," she insisted.

Cutter dipped his head close to hers. "When we get home, Mrs. Gennecut, I'll show you how much fun bad can be."

20

With Vali and Alberto's input, Brash came up with a tentative plan. Once back at Omen Lane, he and Madison shared it with the she-warriors. Together, they tweaked and refined the details.

Brash spent the next day making telephone calls and setting their plans into motion. Granny Bert's friend had finally returned her call and was more than happy to help. Helena promised to do what she could on the homefront. With a plan of this magnitude, it required all the resources they could scrape together. And then some.

After darkness fell, Vali and Alberto came down Mount Perkins. Over a hearty meal, Vali and the she-warriors became immediate friends. All five women shared the traits of tenacity, inner strength, independence, and a wisdom that came only with years of living. Even the language barrier posed little obstacle for a strategy session that lasted past midnight. Optimism floated in the air as the new friends parted.

Tomorrow night, they would implement

justice.

After retiring for the night, Madison gazed over their bedroom window. "Brash? Do you think this is going to work?" Her tone was pensive.

"I certainly hope so." He came up from behind to wrap her in his arms. "Perkins has to be stopped. What he's doing is wrong on every level. It's illegal, immoral, and completely corrupt. He's greedy and without conscience. To him, it's all about money and power. He cares nothing about freedom. Nothing about the people he uses in order to line his pockets."

"Intellectually, I know what Vali and Alberto are doing is wrong. Helping undocumented aliens into our country is illegal. But I can't help from admiring them. Unlike Perkins, they do the wrong thing for the right reason. It has nothing to do with money or greed."

"By Vali's own admission, it does have to do with revenge," Brash reminded her. "Like greed, revenge has a way of coloring a person's better judgment."

"Can you blame her, though? Leaving her behind to die, alone and afraid in the wild? It's unconscionable. And poor Alberto! To cut off his toes! While he was a child, no less. Does Perkins have no compassion at all?"

"Obviously not."

Brash had turned off the light before crossing the room, so there was no glare on the window as they both stared at Mount Perkins. The overhead moon illuminated it with a hazy glow.

The task before them was as monumental as the landform.

"Tomorrow night won't be easy, will it?" Madison knew the answer, but she asked the question anyway.

"No, it won't. It will also be very dangerous. Are you certain you want to go through with this?"

"No, I'm not at all sure," she admitted. "But I don't think we have a choice."

"I'll do everything in my power to protect all of you, but our plan puts everyone at risk. I just want everyone to understand that and be okay with it."

"Granny Bert, Wanda, and Virgie are downright giddy with excitement. They know—and practically welcome— the danger. Miss Sybil is less enthusiastic about the possibly of getting shot, but she's always been one to fight for justice and equality. She'll ignore her own fears for the sake of the greater good."

"I pray it doesn't come to shots being fired. If things go according to plan, we'll avoid any bloodshed. But if I've learned one thing in life—in football, in being a dad, and especially in law enforcement— things don't always go as planned."

"That's true of everyday living. We know the dangers, Brash," she insisted softly. "And we're willing to take the risk. Someone has to stop Perkins."

"I love you, Maddy. I'm proud of your bravery and determination."

"And I love and admire you, more than you know. I have faith this whole scheme is going to work. We make a good team. Together, we can do this."

In reply, he held her close. Tucking his face into the crook of her neck, he breathed in the essence of the woman he loved more than life itself.

After a long moment of silence, Madison nodded toward the mountain. "Now I understand what I mistook as swaying trees," she murmured.

Brash brushed his lips against her hair. "And now I believe the ghost sightings of *La Llorona*."

They were breaking one of Dom's steadfast rules. His instructions were to always have someone at the house during their seven-day, seven-night stay. Madison had followed all his requirements to the letter, except for this one thing.

On this, the seventh night, they left the house unattended. If it forfeited her contract, so be it.

They didn't all leave at once. While Madison and Brash set out on foot toward their destination, Alberto came for the she-warriors one by one. He carried them up the mountain by way of the four-wheeler he borrowed from one of the ranch hands.

Ricardo Reyes, a brother to the man who disappeared almost ten years ago, was now firmly in the 'trust' column. According to Alberto, Ricardo had lived under Perkins' thumb for far too long, terrified he and his entire family would meet the same fate as his brother. Perkins had used that threat against Ricardo often enough, forcing him to cooperate with his evil scheme. Ricardo Reyes would gladly help bring Perkins to his knees.

The she-warriors were thrilled to be a part of the action. Except for Miss Sybil, they were equally thrilled to ride the all-terrain vehicle up the side of the rugged slopes. It was much easier than climbing, they all agreed, and so much faster. Even Miss Sybil insisted that they could scale the mountain if necessary, but the four-wheeler negated the need.

At every bump and every curve, Wanda squealed with glee as she rode behind Alberto. She acted like a girl of eight, rather than a woman of eighty-odd years. She refused to relinquish her seat until he promised to take her again before she left the ranch.

After four trips, all four women were tucked safely in their hiding spot. It was another of the hidden recesses in the side of the rocky formation. This one twisted its way all the way through the mountain, but both entrances were practically invisible to anyone who didn't know of their existence. According to Vali, there were many more like them, and not only on Mount Perkins. Even some of the lower elevations were eroded in a Swiss-cheese fashion. Her favorite passage led down close to the Pecos River. Another wove through the ridges and valleys at the far edge of Dom's property.

"You know plan, sí?" Alberto asked the women.

They all nodded in the affirmative.

With that, Vali wished them well and blended into the shadows of the night. As much as the old woman would love to witness Perkins' downfall firsthand, she had something more important to do. She claimed it was revenge that drove her, but the others could see through her tough facade. Her mission of helping others find freedom was more important to her than settling her own vendetta.

Brash made certain his guns were loaded and tucked into their respective holsters. He did the same for each of the women's weapons. He gathered Madison into his arms, told her he loved her, cautioned the others to stay safe, and slipped out to take his position.

He hid behind a tangle of mesquite brush and cactus. Just before midnight, he heard the roar of an ATV approach from the north. He listened as it wound its way up the flat benches, fought for a grip upon the steepest of inclines, and came to an abrupt halt somewhere just below the mesa's crest.

Leave it to Terrance Perkins to be arrogant enough to believe there was no need for stealth.

A few minutes later, Terrance and Malcolm noisily stomped onto the mountaintop. Brash itched to confront them now, but he knew the importance of waiting. He had to catch Terrance redhanded.

"Norman is on his way up," Terrance said to the other man. Even from here, Brash could hear his lisp. "Get ready."

Malcolm came uncomfortably close to Brash's hiding spot. Stopping on the other side of the brush, the big man dropped two duffel bags and a large messenger-style leather bag into the dirt. Dust rose to tickle Brash's nose, begging him to sneeze.

Time crawled.

Malcolm unzipped the bags in anticipation of filling them.

Terrance obsessively checked his cell phone.

Brash kept low and out of sight, his body coiled like that of a mountain lion.

All three men were impatient for the action to begin.

When Terrance's cell phone lit up, he nodded toward his companion. Malcolm pivoted on the rocky soil and did a poor imitation of an owl's call, directly facing Brash.

Caught off guard, it was all Brash could do not to react. He forced himself to sit still through two ridiculous repetitions before Malcolm turned back around.

Inside the tunnel-like cave, Alberto whispered one word to his companions. "Now."

Madison was the first to come out, with the others not far behind. With the aid of walking sticks and tips from Vali, even the octogenarians navigated the rocky slopes between the cavern and the caprock with success. Their outfits were cumbersome and made the final climb more difficult, but they managed. They kept to the path as instructed and waited in the shadows.

Movement came from the south side of the mountain. Dozens of shuffled feet slugged up the slope, punctuated by grunts and labored breathing.

From behind his cover, Brash saw a huge man appear atop the mesa, leading a string of slow-moving people onto the mesa's crest.

Even bathed in moonlight, the weary

travelers were a sorry sight. They marched in single file, their faces as listless as their exhausted bodies. Their clothing was torn and dirty. Not a single person—not man, woman, nor child—looked as if they chased a dream. They looked more like they faced a guillotine.

Brash didn't miss the weapons strapped to the big man's body, or the AK-47 he held in his arms. Was this Norman, or was this the Hulk that Maddy encountered in town? Larger than Malcolm, he fit her description.

Another man walked among them, herding the group along. He, too, was heavily armed.

The big man barked out orders in Spanish. Loosely translated, Brash knew he told them to pay the man and take a seat. He motioned to Malcolm.

One by one, the illegal immigrants came forward, dropping their payment into the empty bags. Some of them dropped stacks of cash. Some handed over drugs. Even the smallest of children carried small bags of a powdered substance.

Malcolm patted each person down, ensuring they didn't retain any of the contraband for themselves.

It sickened Brash to see the way Malcolm's hands strayed when searching the women. It was all he could do to restrain himself when the man put his filthy hands on the children in the same manner.

Not yet, he scolded himself. He couldn't let his emotions get the better of him. He had to catch Terrance handling the smuggled goods.

Jaw clenched so tightly he thought it might

break, Brash watched as the immigrants turned away dejectedly, only to be met by Terrance. In a brusque tone, he told them to sit in the dirt and empty their backpacks and bags in front of them.

While the last wave of travelers came across the crest, Terrance Perkins strutted smugly among those seated, scowling at their paltry possessions. He shuffled his feet through the contents, mindless of scattering or damaging any goods. His only concern was making certain no one held back on what he considered his to take.

Brash almost lost it when a little girl began to whimper, and Terrance deliberately stepped on her foot. The child's father was seated next to her, his face stoic. He remained silent through her screams of pain. The father knew that any show of resistance would put his entire family at risk.

The little girl's squall was drowned out by another cry, this one long and keening. Despite his outrage at Perkins, Brash had to smile. Madison had excellent timing.

Terrance jerked his head around. The sound was much closer than expected. It normally traveled along the bench just below the mountain's crest.

"Reyes, you fool!" he barked. "Get back where you belong!"

Rather than retreat, the 'ghost' moved forward. Perkins started toward it, preparing to physically rebuke the ranch hand who dared disobey him.

Seeing the ghostly form of *La Llorona* appear from the darkness, the immigrants cried out in fear.

They gasped and curled into themselves. Those with families drew their loved ones close.

Terrance was torn between punishing his worker or pursuing his greed.

Greed won.

Turning back to the crowd, he used whatever force needed to separate the frightened Mexicans. He had already searched half the bags. If one should slip a treasure into a previously checked bag, it would cost him precious time.

"Mendez!" he bellowed over his shoulder. "Make Reyes get back where he belongs."

Mendez was the other man herding the immigrants up the peak and into Malcolm's line for payment. He left the Hulk to handle matters there, stalking toward the sheet-clad body he believed was Ricardo Reyes.

Suddenly, there were two ghosts before him.

Superstitious in his own right, Mendez stopped short.

Seeing the horrific embodiment of two spirits, the terrified Mexicans resisted Terrance. They clung tight to one another, convinced that two *La Lloronas* signaled the ultimate doom. Nothing the American could do to them would be worse than bringing on the wrath of *two* ghosts.

Terrance cursed and kicked, clearly unprepared for their show of defiance. "Norman! Hollister! Someone get over here!"

"Hollister isn't here," the big hulk of a man told him.

The Hulk is Norman Perkins! Brash realized.

The brothers looked nothing alike.

"Not here? Where is he?" The words whistled through Terrance's teeth, but he didn't look over his shoulder. He struggled to tug two women apart, both stronger than he.

"I'm not his keeper," his brother ground out. "He probably stopped to take a leak. He'll be here soon enough."

The normally smooth order of the Perkins' operation disintegrated.

The wailing, now multiplied by two ghosts, grated on Terrance's nerves. "Reyes! Shut the hell up! I have enough racket over here. Norman! Now!"

Norman grumbled about being told what to do, but he went to his brother's aid.

Even in the milky moonlight, Brash could see Mendez's pale face. As the *La Lloronas* continued forward, he backed frantically away, blindly stumbling against anything in his path.

Malcolm was one of those things. In a tangle of arms and legs, he and Mendez both went down hard.

Adding to the melee, a third ghost appeared, and then a fourth. The apparitions came from the other side of the mountain, glowing a ghastly white in the moonlight. The ghosts wailed and cried in the incessant manner of the legendary madwoman.

Terrance jerked around to survey the madness. The few immigrants still standing had dropped to their knees, reciting frantic prayers in Spanish and begging for mercy. But as a fifth apparition appeared, it was more than they could handle. They jumped to their feet and began a mad exodus off the mountain.

Despite his massive size, Norman was caught among them. Two dozen rushing bodies knocked him off his feet and sent him to the ground. His weapons scattered around him, lost amid the trampling herd.

Terrance hesitated for only a moment. With bedlam breaking all around, he knew to cut his losses and make a run for it, but he wasn't about to leave without the duffel bags.

As Terrance grabbed for the bags, Brash sprang into action. He pounced upon him from behind, knocking him into the tangled limbs of Malcolm, Mendez, and two other hapless victims.

Malcolm came up from the pile first, a gun in his hand. Before he could take aim at the lawman, one of the ghosts came close enough to change his mind.

Granny Bert's shotgun cocked close to his ear.

After that, everything happened at once.

Brash's backup arrived with precision timing. Seven armed Texas Rangers, posing at the game ranch as spur-of-the-moment hunters, drew their weapons as a dozen other supporters—some lawmen, some ordinary citizens—swarmed the mountaintop. Led by Granny Bert's old friend and former Justice of the Peace Helena Paul, they blocked any thoughts of escape.

The key to the ATV jingled in Virgie's pocket.

Brash hauled Terrance Perkins to his feet unceremoniously.

"How dare you!" the slighter man blustered. "Do you know who I am?"

"I know *what* you are," Brash spat in return. "Do you know who these gentlemen are?" He nodded to the men wearing camo, their guns trained directly upon him.

"Some of your redneck friends? Washed up has-beens like you?"

Brash didn't let the sneer faze him. "Not in the least. These men are your worst nightmare. These fine men are Texas Rangers, and they're here to arrest you and your brother, and to send you both to prison for a very long time."

"You—You're bluffing." The words whistled with a very pronounced lisp, magnified now with fear.

Two other Rangers, the local sheriff, and one of his deputies forced a bucking, hand-cuffed Norman Perkins into the tight circle around his brother. The senior- ranking Texas Ranger read them their rights and placed them both under arrest.

Hoarse after keeping up the wails of the legendary ghost, the five *La Lloronas* managed a chorus of cheers.

Hollister, the cohort at the back of the caravan, had been intercepted just before cresting the top. Along with Malcolm and Mendez, he was now under heavy guard while awaiting his own arrest.

Even after the five *La Lloronas* shucked their white sheets, one very frightened Mendez continued to eye them warily. Buddy Mendez believed in the power of *La Llorona* and wasn't taking any chances. He turned on his bosses, telling the officials everything.

He said the two brothers had forced him and Ricardo Reyes to do their bidding, threatening their families if they didn't comply. Too frightened to report their illegal operation to the law, the men had unwillingly complied. Reyes played the part of the ghost, while Mendez was forced to be a guide over the rocky terrain. As Norman Perkins' son-in-law Hollister was a willing participant and shared in the profits from their ill-gotten wealth.

By mutual agreement, Alberto stayed in the shadows. Maddy and Brash had no wish to involve him in the matter, nor to risk his freedom. Technically, he was as guilty of smuggling in immigrants as the Perkins were.

The plan also called for Vali to keep her distance, but at the last minute, that plan changed.

After years of seeking revenge (or justice, if one wished to call it that), she couldn't miss this moment.

As the Perkins men were shackled at the ankle like the animals they were, a wild shriek came from the darkness. Another immediately followed, and then another.

Vali, dressed in her flowing garb of all-white and with her wild hair fanning out behind her, seemingly floated at the very edge of the mountainside. Unlike *La Llorona,* she shrieked not for her own lost children but for the countless lost souls these greedy men had misguided. She shrieked for their lost freedoms, and the lost innocence of the children. She shrieked for the many days she spent alone in the rugged land they called America, and for the boy who lost his toes, believing that freedom was within his grasp. She shrieked for her countrymen on both sides of the Rio Grande, and for the cruelty of living under a dictatorship, whether political or financial.

Vali made an ethereal figure as she moved across the ridge. Her eerie cries echoed in the night, sending chills down the spine of all who heard her.

Much like the night of Geraldo Reyes' disappearance, blinding lights appeared in the night sky. Even Vali's mournful shrieks were drowned out by the loud whap-whap-whap of the helicopter's mighty roar. As the chopper landed atop Mount Perkins to collect the handcuffed criminals, Vali vanished into the night.

And just like that, the Perkins reign of tyranny was over.

21

Dom Hebert had finally gotten the messages Virgie left for him and had taken the first flight he could find that serviced the area. He arrived at the ranch the next morning as his guests ate a late breakfast.

"When we finish filling you in, Dom Hebert," Virgie informed him saucily, "I'm going to box your ears! How dare you put us in this sort of danger!"

Dom's mind immediately went to the supernatural. His face turned pale.

"The superstitions are real? Which part? The ghost of *La Llorona,* or the Perkins Curse?"

The four she-warriors answered in unison. "Both!"

"Sit down, Dom," Madison encouraged, "and I'll tell you what we found. Miss Wanda, can you bring another plate? Dom may as well eat while we tell him the long, sordid story."

All smiles, Wanda hurried to fetch a plate and bring it back. "I'll even cook you your favorite meal for supper," she told the man, "right after Alberto takes me for another ride on the four-wheeler. I don't know when I've had such an exciting week!" She clasped her hands together in delight. "And I have *you* to thank for it!"

"Wanda, let the man have some space," Granny Bert told her friend. She couldn't bring herself to chide Wanda too much. In truth, she felt the same way. Despite the dangers, this week had been nothing if not entertaining.

"The so-called Perkins Curse was nothing but a cover-up for two of your cousins' illegal ventures," Madison explained to him. "From what the Texas Rangers have been able to find, only Terrance and Norman were involved in the scheme. Like you, none of the other family members knew what was happening. Norman recruited his son-in-law to help them by cutting him in on the profits, and they coerced a couple of ranch hands to do the grunt work. They used scare tactics and threats to manipulate the men. Then they used rumors of the curse to keep locals away from the ranch, so that no one stumbled upon their secret."

"But that Reyes man, back in '13. How do you explain his disappearance? What about the lights in the sky and the terrible racket like a locomotive?" Dom protested.

"Yeah, about that," said Brash. "It was a helicopter, hovering overhead to do a drug drop. Terrance and Norman have been smuggling in drugs from Mexico for quite a while now. When Reyes stumbled across the drop, they had to silence him. There's no way of knowing what they did with the body or the truck, but they explained his disappearance by reviving the legend of *La Llorona* and creating the Perkins Curse."

Dom used some colorful words to put his own curse on his cousins. Madison wasn't sure, but he may have thrown in a Creole spell or two. With his thick Cajun accent, it was hard to know exactly what he said, but no one doubted his meaning.

After he calmed down enough to work his way into a thick stack of pancakes, he asked, "What about the ghost? People swore they saw her!"

"*La Llorona* played an important part in their hoax," Madison said.

"I do question their logic," Brash was quick to point out, "but they rendezvoused by the full moon. Maybe they thought using flashlights on a dark night would be too obvious. Instead, they used the moonlight to navigate by and tried diverting attention by using *La Llorona* sightings."

Madison took over the story. "Actually, it was Ricardo Reyes under the sheet, the brother of the man who disappeared all those years ago. They threatened that the same would happen to him if he told anyone what they did. Ricardo would travel the highest bench around the mountain in his sheets, calling attention away from what happened on Perkins Ridge."

"What did happen?" Dom breathed, caught up in the story.

"They smuggled in illegal immigrants carrying trafficked guns and drugs." Brash's voice reflected the serious nature of their crime. "The helicopter was too obvious, so they switched to human pack mules. We suspect most of the contraband was provided by Mexican cartels, but that's yet to be proven. Whoever they are, their partners brought immigrants across the Rio Grande where they herded them into a remote holding camp above the Amistad Reservoir. There, gunrunners collected the weapons before escorting the migrants out. To avoid detection, they brought them in small groups, traveling by the moon to meet the brothers at the base of Mount Perkins. We missed the gun exchange, but we witnessed your cousins take possession of the drugs, cash, and whatever contraband brought in. After a normal take, they would launder the money and send a portion back to Mexico in what appeared to be a legitimate business transaction."

"By the way," Virgie added. "While last night's raid was taking place on the mountaintop, a search warrant was carried out at the main ranch. To our knowledge, they're still collecting proof the DA can use against the two brothers."

No one added that, when needed, the Perkins sent select immigrants on for additional drops at other locations. Such was the case with both Vali and Alberto's groups. Their parties were each chosen as these special messengers, and there could be no weak links among them, slowing their deliveries. Alberto's missing toes were not only a mark of his weakness, but a reminder to the others of how they handled defectors.

Yet no matter how cold and inhumane the brother's methods were when dealing with that weakness, the cartel's methods of retribution were far more horrific. If anyone dared not deliver the goods as planned, people lost more than their toes. They lost their life, along with the lives of all their family.

"There's one thing I don't understand," Dom said. "Mount Perkins isn't part of the game ranch."

Brash nodded. "We think they chose this location deliberately. First, it offered them plausible deniability. Wasn't their property, wasn't their fault. Second, they couldn't very well have their hunters stumble across their activities, so they used the land adjacent. And third, Mount Perkins is the highest point for miles around and easily recognized."

"I still don't get how just two of you won against all of them." Dom shook his head in amazement.

"Actually, it wasn't all that many of them," Madison corrected. "Not last night, anyway. I'm sure there were plenty of people involved on the other side of the border and at whatever point they crossed the Rio Grande. Either the gunrunners or someone else brought them as far as the ranch. But the Perkinses kept their circle small. Your cousins were either too stingy to share the profits, too paranoid to trust more than a handful of people, or too arrogant to think they needed help. There were only five of them on Mount Perkins last night, plus a couple dozen illegals." She looked around the table at the she-warriors. "As for us, there weren't just two."

"Not at all," Brash agreed. He nodded to the

proudly beaming ladies. "These four ladies played a big part in the process. We made contact with Reyes and found out he was eager to bring the Perkinses down, so Madison took his place as *La Llorona*. What really confused them was when *five* ghosts appeared! Each of the ladies came out in sheets and played very convincing roles as ghosts."

"Not my first time to do so," Granny Bert pointed out. "You played a roundabout part in it that time, too, Dom."

The man was completely confused by her statement. "Huh?"

"Never mind," Madison said. "And there were plenty of others who helped last night. Granny Bert has a friend who was once the JP here, and she rounded up a posse, of sorts. Brash called the county sheriff and, most importantly, the Texas Rangers. The Rangers posed as game hunters, looking for a last-minute hunt. Since most hunters come on the weekend and leave on Sunday, Terrance jumped at their request to arrive on a Sunday and hunt through the work week. He had no idea they were undercover law enforcement."

"But how did you put it all together? How did you know everything would happen last night?"

"I had my suspicions early on," Brash said, "but I'm the first to admit that I was wrong about what was happening. I suspected they were growing drugs here, not smuggling them in. When Madison found some incriminating evidence, including cash and a marked calendar showing dates and the mark LL—"

"Which we mistook as a Roman numeral two, not the initials of *La Llorona*," she interrupted.

"—we knew it was bigger than a marijuana field."

By mutual agreement, no one mentioned Vali and Alberto, even to Dom. They offered no explanation for the sixth and final ghost on the mountain. Let everyone, even the Rangers, believe it was *La Llorona* herself. Dom's guests admitted nothing of what truly happened behind the scenes.

Greed fueled the Perkinses' operation. By contrast, dreams for a better life fueled Vali's.

The dreamers came to her by word of mouth, seeking a life free of corruption and manipulation. No one could argue that their methods were wrong. They chose to sneak in illegally, something that none of the Americans agreed with, but Brash had said it best. Sometimes, desperation drove people to poor and desperate measures.

The truly desperate, the ones who carried contraband from one country to another, waited near the joining of the two rivers, but Vali's people traveled up the Pecos to meet *angel de la misericordia*. How they reached that point was up to them, but once they crossed onto the very tip of George Perkins' land, Vali took over.

She and Alberto met them at midnight, south of where the game ranch began. From there, Vali led the weary travelers into a long and twisting canyon. She knew the path by heart, crisscrossing in and out of cave-like tunnels and near-hidden holes within the canyon walls. Once through the maze, she took the newcomers to various camps she and Alberto had set up around George's property. After years of living off the land, she knew all the best hiding places. She had lived in some of them herself before discovering her current homesite; the cave on Mount Perkins was by far the best.

She charged only what the travelers could give. A piece of clothing or an offering of food. Sometimes, it was as simple as a heartfelt blessing. Other times, it was something as frivolous as a fancy pair of dancing shoes or an electrical gadget. She had need for neither. But the next person might, so she accepted their offerings in the spirit in which they were given and thanked them for their generosity.

Her flock waited in their camps until she came for them. Alberto made regular rounds to ensure their safety and wellbeing. Occupied with their own venture for the four to five nights the moon was brightest, the Perkins brothers never noticed Vali's movements. On the night of the full moon, she led her followers through the ranch into another twisting tunnel-like canyon and out to chase their American dream.

On the night of the Perkins' downfall, Vali had given one of the travelers explicit directions and asked him to take the lead. She came back to haunt Terrance Perkins one last time.

Not a single person at the table could fault Vali for her compassion, or for her selfless devotion to a cause she believed in. Yes, what she and Alberto did for the immigrants was wrong, but what they did to the Perkins regime was poetic justice. For that, she and Alberto had earned a measure of loyalty.

They had also earned their new friends' silence, but it didn't come without a cost. Brash's generosity to keep them out of trouble came with stipulations.

Over an empty plate, Dom still gushed his praises. "Virgie told me you were the best private eye around. I guess she knew what she was talking about!"

"For the record," Madison corrected, "I'm not a licensed investigator. And you should know that last night, we broke the terms of the contract. We left the house unattended while we were on the mountain."

"You brought down my corrupt cousins, proving the Perkins Curse was a farce and easing my worries about being the thirteenth heir," he pointed out. "I'd say you earned the full amount promised. And to show my appreciation, I'm going to give your assistants here," he motioned to her geriatric sidekicks, "a salary of seven hundred and seventy-seven dollars each. How does that sound, ladies?"

"That sounds like we have a deal!" Wanda said, pumping his hand with pleasure.

"There is one other thing," Miss Sybil informed him rather timidly.

"And what is that?"

"We may have used most of your sheets for our ghost costumes. I'm afraid you're going to need new ones for your beds."

22

They stayed another night at 1313 Omen Lane. There were lingering questions by the Ranger and other officials, and loose ends to tie up.

After Dom's generous offer to pay her in full and to even offer her assistants payment for their help in the case, Madison hated delivering one bit of bad news. She couldn't change the fact that Dom was the thirteenth heir. Those stipulations had been set by Phillip Perkins' will years ago. She couldn't guarantee him that someone wouldn't still try stopping him from claiming his birthright. Even though Terrance, the mastermind behind the smuggling operation, had used superstition to keep his illegal activities secret, she couldn't prove that any of it had been directed toward Dom. The newspaper clippings he received could have been a warning from someone else.

The best she could do was urge him to claim his inheritance as quickly as possible, regardless of superstitions and rumors.

Dom took her advice and set a meeting with

his lawyer for the very next day. When he set out for San Angelo, Brash drove the ladies back to Mount Perkins. They parked at the end of the road and waited for their friends to come to them.

They didn't have long to wait.

"My joints can't take any more climbing," Wanda explained. "Virgie's can't, either, but she's too stubborn to admit it."

Vali offered a rare smile. "No worry. We happy coming to you."

"We brought you a few things," Madison said, offering them the bags.

They had taken only things they knew Dom wouldn't need or miss. A pillow for Vali's bed. One of George's old coats for Alberto. More of his socks and t-shirts. Toiletries and personal items from their own suitcases. One of Granny Bert's sweaters for Vali.

"I'm sorry it has to be this way, Vali," Brash told her. "But you know you can't stay at the cave. You know I can't let you continue bringing in illegal immigrants."

"I know this," she acknowledged. "Alberto and I leave the cave. Thank you for us staying on ranch." She tilted her face into the wind, her wild hair streaming behind her as she stared south. "Others may come still."

"As long as you don't help them," Brash insisted firmly. "New travelers can find the goods on their own."

"*Sí*." She sounded resigned.

Brash forced the younger man to agree, also.

"Alberto?"

"*Sí.*"

"If I ever hear of you breaking your promise, I'll have to report you to the officials," Brash reminded them. "Please, don't make me do that."

"You good man. You not worry. We keep word," Vali assured him. Alberto seconded the notion.

Knowing the Rangers could come back at any time for more evidence, they made their goodbyes brief. It was a bittersweet parting, knowing they would never meet again.

Vali and Alberto's fate was uncertain. Someone could still find them on the ranch and turn them over to Border Security. Some terrible accident or illness could befall them. Their freedom as they knew it could be measured in days.

But wasn't that true of anyone? Madison mused on the long drive home. No one was ever guaranteed tomorrow. But she could learn a lesson from her new friends. Neither had a true house to live in or any means of monetary support, yet they still gave freely to others. They were content with what little they had. Both had overcome tremendous obstacles in life yet didn't allow their misfortunes to define them. They even took this new twist in stride, promising to end their covert operations. They would continue to survive.

It was a valuable lesson to bear in mind.

By the time their group arrived in The Sisters,

it was evening. After dropping off their passengers, Madison and Brash turned toward the Big House.

The moment they opened the door, a delicious aroma welcomed them.

"Welcome home!" all three teenagers told them.

"We made your favorite, Daddy," Megan said. "King Ranch Chicken."

"And one of your favorites, Mom," Bethani added. "Carrot, raisin, and apple salad."

Blake wouldn't be left out. "Hey, don't forget my contribution. I personally picked up a half gallon of Blue Bell Homemade Vanilla ice cream, to go with the chocolate cake Grammy Lydia baked."

Brash rubbed his hands together in anticipation. "It all sounds delicious. I'm starved!"

"Smells yummy, too. Thank you. This is a very welcome surprise." Madison hugged them all again to show her thanks.

Dinner was a noisy affair. The kids were eager to hear about their parents' week, but even more eager to talk about theirs.

"The babies are changing each day," Megan said, clearly enamored with her 'nieces.' "You should see how much little Hope is growing! She had the sniffles but seems better now. And Faith is trying to coo. She sounds so sweet."

"I plan on visiting them tomorrow. How's Genny and Cutter?"

"Poor Aunt Genny," Bethani told her mother, "is beside herself with worry. Myrna Lewis just keeps on. She's determined to pick her to death."

"I talked with Genny on the way home. She said she's not completely certain it's all Myrna. She's worried it goes deeper than the town's number-one nemesis."

"Maybe, but I still say that one way or another, that woman is behind it."

"What about the woman who offered you a job?" Blake asked. "Just because she was nice to you doesn't mean she couldn't be the one causing trouble.

"What job?" Brash asked. "I didn't know you were looking for another job, Bethani."

"I'm not! I love working at *New Beginnings*. But last week, a woman came in with Mrs. Lewis, and even though Mrs. Lewis was her usual complaining self, this woman was really nice. I think it made Mrs. Lewis mad a time or two when she insisted I wasn't as terrible a server as Mrs. Lewis claimed. Anyway, when she left, she left me a nice tip and a note that said she would like me to come work for her in one of her restaurants. She never mentioned that one of those might be here in Juliet, directly competing with Aunt Genny. If that's the case, I would never take the job, no matter what it paid!"

"She's opening a restaurant here? Where?" her stepfather asked. He left for one week, and a new business popped up in town!

"We don't know it's hers, for certain, but we think so. Something is going in next to the grocery store—"

"In the old dry cleaners building." He nodded.

"That's what everyone calls it, but I haven't

lived here for eons like you old-timers," she teased. "I just know it's the building on the corner. They've painted the window sign, and it's called Fresh Start Café. The decal cutouts show pastries, steaming plates, and coffee cups. Aunt Genny said Anastasia Rowland owns several breakfast-themed restaurants in the Houston area."

"Genny does more than breakfast," Madison pointed out. "I'm not sure she has that much to worry about."

"If it was good, honest competition, I don't think she would. But if these attacks on her reputation are how Anastasia Rowland operates, then there's not much about it that's honest."

Megan nodded in agreement. "I'm sure you heard that mean ol' Myrna claims she got food poisoning there and turned Aunt Genny into the health department. Someone else made an anonymous tip a few weeks ago. That Norris guy is threatening to sue. For all we know, Ms. Rowland put them both up to it."

"Hopefully, that's not the case. Norris may just be that sort of guy, and we all know how Myrna is. She'd complain if you hung her with a new rope."

"Sounds promising," Blake muttered.

"Blake! Don't you dare say such a thing!" his mother scolded.

"Fine. Maybe we'll put a curse on her, like the Perkins Curse. We could call it the De-reyn curse."

"De-reyn?"

"You know, deCordova-Reynolds," he said. "De-reyn has a catchier ring to it."

"You doofus," his sister scoffed. "You can't just start a curse. If it were that easy, I'd have put one on you long ago."

"I have you for a twin. Isn't that curse enough?"

"Hardy-har-har. If you were as funny as you looked, I'd be laughing for real."

Ignoring their banter, Megan turned to her stepmother. "But it wasn't really a curse, was it, Mama Maddy? Didn't the Perkins make all that up to scare people away?"

"The curse was all them. They didn't make up the legends of *La Llorona* and *la lechuza*, but they did take advantage of them."

"Tell us about the five *La Lloronas* again," Blake said. "I would love to have seen their faces! I can't believe people thought y'all were actual ghosts!"

"It helped that there was no real light, just the moon. You know how white glows in moonlight. Plus, moonlight makes things look slightly fuzzy and surreal."

"Not only that," Brash added, "but it's part of their culture. I'm sure all of them had heard the legend since they were small children. Even though they may not have believed it as adults, seeing it was another matter."

"Except that it was Mom and the others just acting like ghosts," Bethani pointed out.

"I bet Granny Bert loved that!" Blake grinned, imagining his great-grandmother in all her glory. "She's put together that acting troupe in town. As part of our new community- involvement curriculum, they come to some of our practices for Drama Club. They're even helping with our New Year's Eve Masquerade Ball."

"How's that coming, by the way?" Madison asked.

"Yeah, speaking of the ball..."

Her mom Spidey-sense kicked in. "Uh-oh. Why do I get the feeling that I'm not going to like the next sentence out of your mouth?"

His blue eyes were wide and innocent looking. "I love you, Mom. You don't like hearing that?" Blake did his best to look genuinely hurt.

"You were not just about to say that, and you know it. Not as your next sentence."

"You mean the one where I remind you what a great and supportive mother you are?"

"More like why you feel the need to say such at this particular moment."

"Can't a guy just say good things about his mom?"

"Sure, he can. But we both know you have an ulterior motive in this case. I know this is a drama club we're talking about but cut the act and tell me what's going on."

"Now that you bring it up, I do need a little of that love and support that all moms—especially you— are known for." He swung his doleful blue gaze toward Brash. "I feel especially fortunate to have such a great stepdad that always has my back."

"What favor do you need?" Brash asked, his voice dry.

"Just a little one. It's not like you'll have much to do. We promise to do all the work."

"Who's 'we?'" his mother asked.

"The Drama Club. Granny Bert's crew, too. She thought it was a great idea when I ran it by her!" he said brightly.

Brash looked skeptical. "Why do I already know," he muttered, "that I'm not going to like this?"

Appealing to his mother, Blake gave her his best adoring son look. "You know our big fundraiser is the New Year's Eve Masquerade Ball."

"You may have mentioned it a few hundred times or so," she agreed.

"And you know we were planning to have it at the old theater in Riverton."

'That's what it says on the tickets we've already purchased."

"Yeah, well, now the theater up and sold, and the new owners are taking over immediately. They refuse to honor existing reservations. That means we have no place to hold our ball."

"If you're worried we want our money back, forget it. Consider it a donation."

"That's not it."

"What is it, then?"

"I sort of volunteered the Big House as the new venue."

"You what?" Madison cried.

"Actually, Granny Bert gave me the idea. She was talking about the balls she used to attend here at the house, back in the day. The entire third floor used to be a ballroom."

"Yes, I know that. And you know that it's now your sisters' bedrooms."

"But the huge space in between is our rec room. It's actually most of the old ballroom, in fact. It wouldn't be all that hard to move stuff out of the way and have the party up there. And if it's not big enough, we have plenty of rooms downstairs for overflow."

"If you had bothered consulting me," his mother said, "I would have pointed out that New Year's Eve is only six or seven weeks away. Not nearly long enough to plan a party of this magnitude!"

"It's not a party, exactly. And we'll do all the planning, and all the work."

She crossed her arms skeptically. "Somehow, I highly doubt that."

"We will, I swear. Please, Mom? Please, Daddy D? We're desperate. If we can't find a place this week, our teacher says we have to call the whole thing off. We've already put so much time and effort into it. All we need is a place to hold it. That's all."

"I don't know, son. This is a lot to ask," Brash said.

"And at a terrible time!" his mother wailed. "I've barely started my Christmas shopping. Then I have to wrap, decorate, plan menus, and do all my cooking. What about your Cookie Campaign? Do you plan to carry on your tradition?"

"Of course!" all three teens answered.

"We're already signing up volunteers," Bethani added. "This promises to be the best year yet."

Blake tried a new tactic. "Think of it this way. Now you don't have to worry about what you'll do for New Year's Eve." He flashed his best showman's smile.

"Nice smile, but I wasn't worried. We already bought tickets, remember?"

"But without a venue, they're useless. Come on, Mom. This is my last year in high school. One of the last times you can really come through for me while I'm still in school."

"That's low, Blake."

"I know," he said sheepishly, bowing his blond head. He looked at her through his eyebrows. "But is it working?"

His look reminded her so much of his antics as a mischievous little boy, that Madison couldn't help but laugh. She fell for his contrite expression and charming smile every time!

For the record, she reiterated, "I still don't like that you did this without asking us first."

The teen placed his hand over his heart. "And for that, I am truly sorry. Please forgive me."

"A bit of overkill there, Blakey, but I do accept your apology. So, if it's okay with your father, I suppose it's okay with me. If you do all the work."

"We will, I swear." He turned to Brash. "Daddy D? You won't let me down, will you?"

"You do realize I've heard every con there is. My players used to come to me with all sorts of wild tales and excuses. Criminals are even more creative. Your line of bull doesn't work as well on me, but I do agree with your mother. If you and your club promise to do all the work, and all we have to do is provide the location, then, yes, I guess it's okay with me."

Blake was all smiles. His fist shot into the air.

"Yes! You guys are the best parents in the world! I swear, we'll do everything. All you have to do is sit back and relax and enjoy the ball." He fell back in his chair, still beaming with pleasure. "I'm telling you. This will be one New Year's Eve you'll never forget!"

Please join us again in late December for another unforgettable mystery in The Sisters, *Murder at the Stroke of Midnight!*

As always, I'm honored you've chosen to read my story and appreciate you more than you know. If you're so inclined, please tell a friend about my books. Public reviews on Amazon, BookBub, Goodreads, Facebook, and other sites are the lifeblood of any author.

Like most of my tales, this story was inspired by personal experience, admittedly secondhand. A few years ago, my husband hunted in an area near the fictional town of Manhattan. He witnessed illegal immigrants traveling across the ridges of mountaintops. Sometimes, he only heard their voices. Another time, my son had a close encounter with illegal aliens who broke into the camp where he stayed. (He had an even closer encounter with a rattlesnake!) To this day, friends who own property near the southern border of Texas leave out coolers of water and drinks to deter break-ins. I used these personal insights not for political reasons, but as inspiration for the storyline.

Also, even though my stories often stem from personal experiences, I'm pleased to report that none of those extend to murder, or to Madison's habit of finding dead bodies!

I'll meet you back in The Sisters with *Murder at the Stroke of Midnight*.

Note:

I hesitated when using the word 'mountain.' Texas isn't home to majestic ranges like the Rocky Mountains, but we do have a few impressive formations. I'm sure someone will correct me on the proper definition of a mountain (which, by the way, is a landform that rises at least one thousand feet above its surrounding area, which this area is known to have), so please humor me.

ABOUT THE AUTHOR

Becki Willis, best known for her popular The Sisters, Texas Mystery Series and Forgotten Boxes, always dreamed of being an author. In November of '13, that dream became a reality. Since that time, she has published numerous books, won first place honors for Best Mystery Series, Best Suspense Fiction and Best Audio Book, and has introduced her imaginary friends to readers around the world.

An avid history buff, Becki likes to poke around in old places and learn about the past. Other addictions include reading, writing, junking, unraveling a good mystery, and coffee. She loves to travel, but believes coming home to her family and her Texas ranch is the best part of any trip. Becki is a member of the Association of Texas Authors, the National Association of Professional Women, and the Brazos Writers organization. She attended Texas A&M University and majored in Journalism.

You can connect with her at http://www.beckiwillis.com/ and http://www.facebook.com/beckiwillis.ccp?ref=hl. Better yet, email her at beckiwillis.ccp@gmail.com. She loves to hear from readers and encourages feedback!